Madoc's
Prickly Problem

Celia Lucas

PONT BOOKS

First Impression – 2000

ISBN 1 85902 777 6

The author wishes to acknowledge the award of the Irma
Chilton bursary from the Arts Council of Wales for the
purpose of writing this book. It is also published with the
support of the Arts Council of Wales.

Printed in Wales at
Gomer Press, Llandysul, Ceredigion

For Lol
because he loves animals
and arrived too late for the earlier stories

PLAS NEWYDD
LLANFAIRPWLL
ANGLESEY
LL61 6DZ

MADOC'S PRICKLY PROBLEM

Celia Lucas's fantasy cat world of goodies
and baddies set in the real North Welsh
world is both convincing and witty. This
latest story, like its predecessors, is
thrillingly exciting and brilliantly written.

The Marquess of
Anglesey

Chapter One

Horatio Hedgehog uncurled his prickles and looked about nervously.

'That was a near miss,' he said to himself. 'I must be more careful in future.'

Horatio had just crossed a busy main road. It was night-time, when hedgehogs do most of their running about, and the car had come over the brow of the hill at such a pace that Horatio hadn't even noticed the beam of the headlights until the rubbery black wheels were just millimetres from his spines. He had immediately curled himself up into a ball, of course, and rolled to the side of the road, but it was a nasty moment.

On his journey from his home village of Llanystumdwy, near Cricieth in north Wales, up to Caernarfon, which he had just by-passed, he had witnessed many tragedies among his fellow hogs. Sad squashed remains, carrion for crows, littered the highways. Motherless young hogs starved in the hedgerows, and garden hogs didn't fare much better. Horatio shuddered at the memory of what the electrically-powered cutter humans called a strimmer had done to his best friend, Huw. It had come at him in his hedge on a summer evening, roaring like a lion, and chopped his front legs clean off. If it hadn't been for Jane, the kind lady from the Welsh Hedgehog

Hospital, he'd have been chasing slugs in that Great Hoggery in the Sky. Instead of which he was living a life of luxury in Jane's Rehabilitation Centre in Aberystwyth, with his legs sewn back on so skilfully that he scarcely could believe they had once parted company with the rest of him.

Yes, the scientific age could work wonders, thought Horatio, but what with traffic, pesticides and strimmers, and now this new threat to their existence, was the twenty-first century really the place for a hog?

'A penny for them,' squeaked a high-pitched voice from the undergrowth behind him.

'For what?' asked Horatio, peering through the thick grass to see what sort of creature had addressed him.

'Your thoughts, of course. Except that I haven't got a penny. Not even half a pound of tuppenny rice. Pop!'

'Ooh, squeal, what's that?' Horatio jumped at the sudden explosion of sound. Surely it wasn't some form of midnight strimmer on the rampage?

'Pop!' There it was again. 'Pop goes the what?'

'The what?' asked Horatio, thoroughly confused and still unable to see where the voice was coming from. He raised his head and sniffed the air in a characteristically hoglike attitude.

'Pop goes the weasel, of course,' said the voice. 'Wilbert Weasel, that's me. At your service.'

Wilbert Weasel emerged, snakelike, from the long grass. He was about 25 centimetres long and had a beautiful reddish brown 'top coat' and a snow-white under-belly. His legs were short and his feet fine and delicate, not unlike Horatio's own dainty footfalls. 'Chilly for the time of year,' he remarked, amicably.

'Yes, it's been cold ever since I came out of hibernation two months back,' said Horatio. 'Some of these nights, when I've had my fill of slugs and other tasty morsels, I'd just as soon curl up in a snug hedge, but I am on an important mission and time is of the essence.'

'What sort of mission?' asked Wilbert. 'You can trust a weasel with any secret but never a stoat.'

'Why not a stoat?' asked Horatio.

'Because stoats are s-totally different. See?'

'I suppose so,' said Horatio. But somehow the exchange had made him decide not to trust weasels either. You couldn't be too careful these days.

'I'm heading for the Isle of Anglesey, Ynys Môn,' he said instead. 'The town of Beaumaris, in fact. Is it far, do you know?'

'Yes and no,' replied Wilbert enigmatically.

As he talked, Wilbert darted to and fro, a bit like a terrestial eel, making Horatio feel quite giddy. 'What do you mean, yes and no?' he squeaked, trying not to

follow Wilbert's movements with his eyes. To be sick now would be most undignified, not to say a waste of those tasty spiders he'd found in the corner of a shed earlier that evening.

'Yes, if you're walking, and no, if you hitch a lift,' said Wilbert. 'Why do you want to go there anyway?'

Horatio thought for a minute and removed a few irritating fleas from between his prickles. There could be no harm in telling Wilbert whom he wanted to see. It was just the problem itself, the terrible threat that hung over his entire species, that he should keep quiet about. He must take no chances. If a way of dealing with it could be found, then the fewer animals who knew about it the better.

'I want to see Madoc the Magnificent, trilingual leader of the Steel Town Cats,' said Horatio. 'I'm told he helps animals in distress.'

'Then you've met just the right weasel,' said Wilbert. 'It so happens that Miss Kip, the golden greyhound, the best friend of the Steel Town Cats, is staying at this moment on my farm with her human, Sam. They'll give you a lift when they leave for Beaumaris tomorrow.'

'So I don't need to walk all that way after all?' said Horatio. He had been extremely worried about how he would get over either of the two bridges that link Ynys Môn to the mainland without being seen and perhaps captured. He might even be thrown into the waters of the Menai Strait by a late night reveller.

'No, of course you don't,' said Wilbert. 'Just come

home with me. I'll introduce you to Miss Kip and Bob's your uncle.'

'Well, actually, he isn't,' said Horatio, not wishing to appear dishonest. 'His name's Hywel, Hywel Dda, Hywel the Good, and he's one of the unfortunate hogs that . . .' He bit his lip to stop himself continuing. 'Ouch,' he said, 'sorry, I mean . . . I'm in a right prickle, I mean pickle, I mean . . .'

'Never mind,' said Wilbert, standing upright now on his hind legs, displaying his handsome white bib and stomach. 'Come on.'

The two animals burrowed through the hedge and, leaving the busy road, set off across a field towards the farmhouse. The moon lit their way. Some dozing cows mooed as they passed, a barn owl hooted.

Wilbert was faster than Horatio, and quieter in his movements. After a while he realised that Horatio was no longer following him. Surely the owl wouldn't have attacked him? No, that was unlikely. He got up on his hind legs and started a high-pitched trill. 'Horatio, io, io! Where are you, i-you, i-you?'

His sensitive ears pick up a snuffle, then a snort. Horatio had his snout in a pat of cow dung and was foraging for grubs.

'No time for that now,' said Wilbert. 'I thought you wanted my help.'

'I do, I do,' Horatio assured him. 'I just couldn't resist that nice, soft, slimy, beautifully formed. beetle-infested, brown, glowing . . .'

'Come on,' said Wilbert. 'I'm getting bored.'

Helping Horatio had seemed interesting at first but weasels have a short attention span and quickly want to move on to something else.

'All right,' said Horatio, 'but before we go, can you just put me right on one thing that's been bothering me?'

'What's that?' asked Wilbert.

'Why are stoats s-totally different?'

'Because, silly, they have a dirty black tip on the end of their tails. You're not very observant, are you?'

'No, I suppose not,' said Horatio, whose sight, in common with the rest of his species, was not his strong point. 'Thanks for the information.'

'And we common weasels have a highly distinguishing mark. I don't suppose you've noticed that either?'

'Well, I can't say . . . I'm afraid . . .' began Horatio.

'No, of course you haven't. We common weasels – I use the term "common", by the way, not to indicate social inferiority but to give us our official name: it means we are the main sort of weasel around. Anyway, to return to our distiguishing mark . . .'

'Yes?' squeaked Horation.

'We common weasels, as opposed to snow weasels, have a brown cheek spot.'

'A sort of beauty spot?' asked Horatio.

'Well, yes, you could say that,' said Wilbert, flattered.

'Anyway, hence the saying: a weasel is w-easily distinguished but a stoat is s-totally different.'

'I see,' said Horatio, and this time he thought he really did. 'Are we nearly there?'

'Yes, if you can keep your mind off food,' said Wilbert. 'There'll be plenty when you get to Beaumaris, lots of gardens choc-a-bloc with caterpillars. The humans will be glad to see you, I would think. The gardener's friend, they call you, don't they?'

They reached the farmyard. The May night was nearly over. Already the moon was paling in the sky and the stars were losing their brightness.

'They get up early so it won't be long before Miss Kip comes out to stretch her paws and raise her tail,' Wilbert assured Horatio. 'I'll have a word with her and she'll see you all right. Pop!'

'Goes the weasel!' Horatio completed the line. 'Meanwhile, if you don't mind, I'll have a little snooze in this newly mown grass. Smells delicious.'

'Right, see you later, alligator!'

Horatio was too tired to protest that he wasn't in the least like an alligator. Except that he could swim well. He burrowed into the soft grass, gave a sigh of contentment and settled down.

In a few hours he would be able to confront Madoc with his Prickly Problem and all would be well.

Chapter Two

Madoc the Magnificent was bored. He yawned, exposing a fine set of sharp, feline teeth. A starling caught his eye and his ears pricked. He followed the movement of the bird with his deep amber, unblinking eyes. Should he adopt the crouching position of the practised hunter: the purposeful movement of the tail, the haunches that quivered in anticipation of lift off? No, he could not be bothered. He turned away from the bird, blinked, and yawned again.

The problem was that Madoc, trilingual leader of the Steel Town Cats, was on too comfortable a wicket. Some cats, most you could say, enjoy nothing better than lazing around in the sun or by a nice warm fire, taking occasional refreshment and purring when their humans seem to require it. But Madoc, magnificent, indeed, in size, in the shininess of his sleek black coat and especially in the length and curl of his dazzling white whiskers, was an animal who longed for action. He had been a worker cat all his life. Before they closed down, he had been chief ratter and mouser at the steelworks on Deeside, in north Wales. Then, after various adventures, he had been commissioned by the prime minister, no less, to rid Britain's offshore islands of vermin. His own group had been so successful on Puffin Island, known in Welsh as Ynys Seiriol, just off the coast of

Beaumaris, that it required only a handful of mousers now to keep the situation under control. Madoc himself, along with his most trusted companions, had secured a longterm mousing contract with the Council in Beaumaris town.

It was a good, steady job and Madoc was grateful. Of course he was. But cats cannot live by mice alone. He needed a challenge. Something that would exercise his brain as well as his considerable physical powers.

He got up and stretched himself, arching his powerful back and extending first his front and then his back legs, so that his lithe body looked like a roller-coaster. His snow-white waistcoat caught the morning sunlight and the white tips of his paws gleamed against the contrasting black of his legs.

'The public will be coming in soon,' he thought to himself. 'I'll just patrol the ramparts while I've got a few minutes.'

Madoc had been doing his contemplating inside the inner ward, or bailey, of Beaumaris Castle, an ancient edifice built by King Edward I in 1295. This castle was now his home. He and his feral gang had made snug dens amidst the stonework where they could be dry and warm in winter and cool in summer. Half wild, they did not crave the security of a domestic situation. They might visit, yes, but stay never, or hardly ever. The castle was ideal and, in addition, a royal residence seemed only right and proper for one as splendid as Madoc the Magnificent.

Although a ruin, there was enough of the castle left standing to imagine how it might have been when garrisoned by the English invaders, and ultimately conquerors, all those centuries ago. From the watchtowers the guard would have spotted marauders approaching by land or sea; in the dining hall minstrels and bards would have entertained great lords and ladies; in the chapel Mass would have been said daily.

And the rats and mice! Ah, those were the days, thought Madoc, when rat poison was unknown and a cat's worth was fully appreciated.

He turned into a stone doorway and scampered up the steep, spiral staircase, also built of stone. Narrow apertures in the wall, from which arrows could be fired, gave some light to the dark interior. At last he emerged into bright sunlight and the pupils of his eyes, which had been large, black and round in the darkness, narrowed to slits. The wind from the sea ruffled his coat and whistled through his whiskers.

He shook himself, turned to give his fur a reassuring lick and jumped up on to the parapet wall. He was high above the town now. The townspeople had grown used to the strange sight of a cat patrolling their castle ramparts. Some had been worried at first that he would fall to a certain death in the moat hundreds of metres below, but cats are more sure-footed than humans, with a better sense of balance, and Madoc hardly needed to look down at all as he pranced, paw before gleaming paw, along his precarious highway.

At 10 o'clock the public would be allowed in, and

since it was fine weather and a weekend, many visitors were expected. Madoc would disappear before then.

The bells of the church of St Mary and St Nicholas told him it was nine o'clock. He sat down on his haunches by one of the castle's turrets and gazed out at his domain. Surely this must be the most beautiful place in the world? Across the Menai Strait, the narrow channel of water that separates the Isle of Anglesey from mainland Wales, stretched, in panoramic wonder, the mountains of Snowdonia. It was late May but Snowdon, the highest mountain in England and Wales, still kept its white, snow-capped tip. To his left paw, across the sea that was called Liverpool Bay, rose the huge mound of the Great Orme, where, 4,000 years ago, a busy settlement of people and animals had lived and flourished. Behind him, green fields, dotted with sheep and lambs, climbed up in a gentle slope towards Baron Hill.

What a fortunate animal he was. And yet . . .

The sound of a familiar bark caught his ear. He looked down to the swan-dotted moat below and beyond to the pathway which led to the main entrance. There, trotting briskly, on elegant paws, was a golden greyhound, ears pricked, eyes alert. She was followed, at a slower pace, by a curious brown lump of something.

'Bark,' said the golden greyhound, 'Bark, bark!'

'Miss Kip!' exclaimed Madoc. 'I'm here, I'm coming, miaoooow!'

Madoc's miaow of greeting was so loud and

19

penetrating that it carried down clearly to the animals below. In the street, Trevor Baker dropped a tray of buns he was carrying into his bakery. 'Bother that cat,' he said with unaccustomed mildness for an ex-Naval man.

'He'll be here before you can say "Kippers",' Miss Kip told her companion, who, at the sudden noise, had curled himself into a ball. 'He'll sort things out for you, I know he will.'

Madoc ran to greet Kip with happy little 'brrrrp' sounds. Kip wagged her tail with the vigour of an over-excited windscreen wiper. She sniffed at Madoc's face with her shiny black nose and licked him all over.

'May I introduce Horatio Hedgehog?' she said when the greetings were done. 'He's got a problem he's hoping you can help him with.'

'A prickly problem, no doubt,' said Madoc, viewing the burr-like ball before him.

'Come on, Horatio, uncurl yourself,' barked Miss Kip. 'Here's Madoc the Magnificent, prince among animals.'

Since the castle would soon be crowded with visitors, the animals decided to go back to Kip's garden to discuss plans. The other Steel Town Cats, or most of them, would be there anyway by now receiving their customary morning saucers. After that, a quiet nap beneath the apple tree was always welcome or, in inclement weather, in Sam's cosy shed.

Miss Kip lived with a proper family just a few paw lengths from the castle. The family comprised Sam and his wife and four children. Tessa, aged twelve, a fair-haired girl with freckles, was her best friend and she loved her dearly. Tessa loved Kip in return. She was responsible for feeding her and brushing her coat so it always shone soft gold.

'Come on, Horatio, climb on my back,' said Kip, sitting down to allow Horatio to clamber up, 'it'll be quicker this way.' They reached the house in a couple of minutes and went straight through to the back garden, where, as they'd expected, a posse of cats was assembled. They ran to greet Madoc and Kip with welcoming miaows but drew back when they saw the strange prickly thing riding Kip's back.

'It's all right, cats,' said Madoc. 'It's only Horatio Hedgehog. He's come to tell us about his prickly problem, so let's all settle down and hear what he has to say.'

The cats gathered round: Patchwork, Madoc's right-paw cat, Esmerelda the Efficient, the grey with the worried question-mark of black fur over her left eye, Marmaduke, the wise elder statescat, and his great-nephew Scarper Purr Kitten. Marmaduke and Scarper were not Steel Town worker cats: they lived as domestic animals in the house next door. Both were ginger and white with spectacular white whiskers, an attribute of their famous family, The Purrs of Pontybodkin. On his back left leg Scarper – so called because he was always running off – besported a garter of snow white fur.

'So tell me everything, Mr Hedgehog,' said Madoc. 'Leave out no details. Straight as a porcupine's quill, if you please.'

'Well, it's been a chilly spring on the whole, more like hibernation weather,' Horatio began. He wasn't good at getting straight to the point and he resented Madoc's reference to porcupines. Surely he, of all animals, knew that porcupines were horrid rodents not in the least like insect-eating hedgehogs? His spines bristled with irritation but he controlled himself and continued: 'A distinct nip in the air there's been. Many's the night I've thought of returning to my nest, I can tell you . . .'

'Lazy bundle of prickles!' mewed Scarper,

'sleeping all winter and then wanting to go back for more.'

'Quiet, you impertinent kitten,' said Esmerelda, and biffed him with her paw.

'I find that remark most offensive,' said Horatio, unable to stomach a second insult. 'I am extremely UP-set.' He emphasised the 'up'.'Hibernation is not at all the same thing as sleeping, not at all. I've a good mind to curl up and say no more.'

'As you please, Horatio, but you're the one who's asking for help, remember,' said Madoc. 'I know Scarper was rude but he's only a kitten and he doesn't understand. Indeed, I'm not sure I do. Why *do* you hibernate and what is the difference between that and sleeping?'

'Well,' said Horatio, 'it's like this. You sleep to restore your energy and wake up refreshed for the next day but when you hibernate you save your energy altogether. In hibernation we cool our bodies down so much that we hardly need to heat them at all. Then, because we're so cold, everything slows down, breathing, heartbeat, growth, digestion. It's suspended animation, I suppose.'

'It sounds awfully boring,' said Scarper, 'not doing anything for months and months.'

'Well, it's not boring if you don't know you're doing nothing, if you see what I mean.' Horatio was getting confused again.

'But why?' mewed Scarper. 'What's the point? The winter can be so lovely with the snow on your paws and the frost on your whiskers and a nice warm fire in your human's house.'

'Nice for some, perhaps, but not for hogs. By November nearly all our food supply has gone, beetles, worms and so on. Hibernation is a very efficient alternative to starvation.'

'Don't you eat at all in the winter, then?' mewed Scarper. 'No Christmas turkey? No mince pies and Christmas pudding?' He had enjoyed his first Christmas last year.

'Nothing,' said Horatio. 'That's why we eat so much in the summer, to store up fat that will keep us alive until the next spring.'

'And what happens if you haven't stored up fat, if you're still small and skinny?' asked Scarper, concerned. He was a plump kitten but he had friends who were scrawny.

'Ex-hog,' said Horatio. 'If you're under 1 lb, that's 450 grams, in weight you're for that Great Hoggery in the Sky. Fortunately I've never had that problem . . .'

'I can see that!' mewed Scarper.

'Quiet, you bad kitten,' said Esmerelda, and raised an admonitory paw.

'Well, thank you, Horatio, for your explanation,' said Madoc. 'Now please may we have your story?'

'As I observed,' said Horatio, 'the weather had been unseasonably chilly but three weeks ago, the 1st of May it was, we had a pleasant spell and our colony of hogs came out to enjoy the balmy evening before setting out on a night's foraging. Suddenly we heard the sound of engines and before you could say "Woodlouse" two men had jumped out of a van and were scooping us up by the prickleful and throwing us into crates.

'Every so often they would find a reject – poor old Uncle Hywel, weak little Hermione – and they'd pick them up and fling them out. Hermione didn't survive the shock. I found her later, gasping for breath, on her way to that Great Hog in the Sky.'

'But how could they pick you up with all those prickles?' mewed Scarper. 'I hurt my paw just trying to be friendly.'

'Heavy duty gloves. Oh, they came prepared all right,' said Horatio, and emitted a curious squealing sound, not dissimilar to a frightened pig. It was the memory of that terrible evening that alarmed him so.

'Correct me if I'm wrong,' said Madoc, 'but I understood hedgehogs to be solitary animals. How was it that there were so many of you together?'

'Well, it's particularly good foraging round there. Llanystumdwy beetles are well known as a delicacy throughout the hedgehog world and the earthworms are juicy beyond belief. And the spiders – great fat, black bodies with legs the size of . . .'

'Do you mind?' miaowed Esmerelda. 'I don't like spiders.'

'And, of course,' added Horatio, 'it is the mating season.'

'Quite,' said Madoc. 'I must ask, however, how you managed to escape?'

'I was lucky,' said Horatio. 'I was right on top of the crate where they had stuffed about thirty of us, packed together like thorns on a gorse bush. One of the men was trying to shut the crate when I saw a patch of pink skin showing through on his wrist. I rolled over and aimed my prickles right at it. I must have struck a main artery as the blood spurted out and he swore something horrible.'

'Swore horribly,' corrected Great Uncle Marmaduke, who was something of a pedant in the matter of grammar. He had been catnapping during the explanation on hibernation, which he knew all about anyway, but now he was all ears.

'Anyway,' continued Horatio, raising and flattening his prickles in annoyance, 'his attention was diverted and I was able to roll myself out of the crate and into the bushes where I hid until the noise died down.'

'And the others?' asked Madoc.

'Driven away the Great Hog knows where and only myself and old Uncle Hywel left to tell the tale. Mother, father, brothers, sisters, friends, all gone. And little Hermione dead by my snout.'

'Terrible,' said Patchwork. 'A cruel story.' And he attempted to lash the stump that was his tail, the rest having been bitten off in an unfortunate encounter with a Staffordshire bull terrier.

'Did you get any clues as to the identity of these humans?' asked Madoc. 'The number of their van? Their names? Their accents? Think hard, Horatio, hogs' lives depend on your answers.'

'Well, there was something but it's hardly worth mentioning.'

'What?' miaowed Madoc.

'The man who I pricked . . .'

'Whom,' corrected Marmaduke. 'Whom I pricked. The man is the object of the sentence and . . .'

'Please, Marmaduke Purr, I know you're a scholarly animal and know a lot more about grammar and words and spelling than any of us uneducated animals but please allow Horatio to tell his story in his own way. It's the truth we seek, not a GCSE pass in semantics, whatever those may be . . .'

'The meanings in language,' said Marmaduke, not to be put down.

'Right,' said Madoc, turning to Horatio, 'now we've sorted that out, pray continue, Mr Hedgehog, with your narrative.'

'The man whom I pricked,' said Horatio in a rather peevish squeak, 'had a funny smell. It was something he was chewing. A smell I know well from the woods but the shock of the incident has wiped the name clean from my memory. It was g . . . g . . .'

'Gammon,' mewed Scarper. His human had given him a morsel of that last night. He purred at the memory of the sharp, salty taste and licked his lips.

'Don't be a silly kitten,' miaowed Esmerelda the Efficient, giving him a cuff with her paw. 'You don't find gammon in the woods.'

'Well, you might find pigs there . . .' began Scarper.

'Not cooked, cured and smoked pigs in slices,' said Esmerelda. 'And don't answer back, you impertinent kitten. Speak when you're spoken to.'

'Silence,' growled Madoc. 'Was there anything else, Horatio? I hope I may call you that?'

'Squeak,' agreed Horatio. 'There was so much noise and shouting and squealing I didn't hear much,' he continued, 'and hedgehogs go into shock, you know, in a crisis. I was dazed most of the time, honest.'

'But you had enough presence of mind to put a prickle in that man's wrist. Come on, Horatio, if you want us to help you, you must try and help us. What about Uncle Hywel? Did he have anything to say?'

Gradually the parting words of Uncle Hywel Dda came back to Horatio.

'I'm an old hog, that's why they threw me out,' he told his nephew. 'It's obvious, for some reason we have yet to elicit, that they want young, strong hogs. That's why poor sickly Hermione was no use to them either. If mass hogicide was their intention, a couple more bodies, whatever their condition, would have been a bonus. No, they need healthy hogs for a purpose. Scientific research, perhaps, or maybe to sell them to humans in a hogless land. We won't be the only colony to be attacked in this way, mark my words. Go to Madoc the Magnificent, my boy, and save our species from extinction.'

With a great effort the old hog continued:

'It's too late for me, I'll soon be gone to the Great

28

Hoggery in the Sky, but fight for future generations. Try, with Madoc, to get protection for our species, human laws that will make it a crime to treat us in this way. Things are better than they were, I know, in this respect but laws can be tightened and punishments increased. Go, my boy, and may your prickles protect you!'

Madoc listened in silence to Horatio's account of his uncle's words. He was crouched on the grass, his front paws, black with white tips, just visible beneath the thick fur of his white waistcoat. Paws showing is the concentrating position; paws tucked under indicates repose. The other cats followed his example.

'He's right, there must be a purpose,' said Madoc. 'And where humans are involved there's probably financial gain, or hope of financial gain, anyway.'

'Money is the root of all evil,' growled Marmaduke.

'Quite,' said Madoc. 'Which is why we animals don't use it.'

'But be fair, *chwarae teg*,' barked Miss Kip, 'we may not use money ourselves but we don't mind our humans spending it on us, do we?' A loyal hound, she was always ready to stick up for her human family.

'We digress,' said Madoc sternly. 'Let us stick to the matter in hand. Names, Horatio. Surely you heard a name mentioned, or a town, or district, or a date even?'

'The 31st. Me birthdai!'

'My . . .' began Marmaduke, but he was silenced by a glare from Madoc's amber eyes.

'I mean, that's what he said,' squeaked Horatio. 'The man who was crating me up, the one with that smell. Now I remember. And that's how he said it, with that accent. It sounded all funny to us Welsh hogs. One man, who was Welsh like us, said, "See you on the 31st, Alf." And the man I pricked, Alf, I suppose, answered, "The 31st, me birthdai".'

'So we have one Welshman and another man, Alf, who sounds like a Cockney from London,' said Madoc. 'Well done, Horatio, that's a good start.'

'Oh, now it's coming back to me,' squeaked Horatio, encouraged by Madoc's praise. 'The Welshman's name was Gwilym. Alf made some stupid joke about "Squeal 'em, Gwilym". Poor Hermione, she didn't have a chance.'

'Hermione! What a silly name for a Welsh hedgehog,' whispered Scarper Purr Kitten to his friend Twm Cati who had just joined them.

'Horatio's no better,' mewed Twm. 'Must all be above themselves in Llanystumdwy just because a prime minister lived there.'

'Silence, you two,' growled Esmerelda, and raised a threatening paw. In the cause of greater efficiency she had taken upon herself the task of keeping kittens in order. Patchwork came forward to have his miaow. 'And what about the 31st?' he asked. 'Lots of months have 31sts. Let's see, 30 days hath September, April, June and . . .'

'No, Patchwork, don't you see, it must be May 31st,' said Madoc. 'It was May when the incident happened so Gwilym had no need to name the month. It was obvious. If it had been July or August he'd have said "See you July 31st" or "See you August 31st". It's elementary, my dear Patchwork.'

'And today's the 21st,' said Esmerelda, 'so we've got ten days.'

'Garlic,' miaowed Marmaduke, and leapt to his paws amazingly swiftly for an elderly cat.

'What?' barked, mewed and squeaked the animals. 'Garlic, that's what Horatio smelt. It grows wild in the woods so he would know the smell well. This man, this Alf, was chewing garlic.'

'Well done, Marmaduke, now we've got a lot to go on,' said Madoc. 'Names, a date, a smell. We must call a full Council of Cats and put a plan into action.'

Chapter Three

The full Council of Cats met that afternoon in Miss Kip's back garden. Present were Madoc's right-paw cat Patchwork, so called because of his coat of many colours, Esmerelda the Efficient, elder statescat Marmaduke and Scarper Purr Kitten. Also in attendance were Snowy Tom, Geraint Growler, Twm Cati, twins Susie and Sailor and Carlo the Caterwauler, accompanied by members of his choir. Carlo's caterwaulers were known throughout the cat world for the penetrating quality of their yowls, which had won many prizes at Eisteddfodau all over Wales. Carlo conducted his caterwaulers with his white right paw, the only bit of white on his otherwise coal-black coat.

Snowy Tom, an original member of the Steel Town Cats, had been away for some months working as deputy mouser at a Motorway Service Station. He'd been attracted to the job by the promise of frequent snacks, for food was everything to Snowy. But although the leftovers were tasty and there were plenty of them, he found the place noisy and comfortless and his immediate boss, Rufus the Ratcatcher, expected far too much of him in the way of mousing quotas. When he heard that Madoc had moved from windswept Puffin Island to a cosy castle in a pretty and prosperous town, he took the next lift going north-west.

'Sorry, Rufus, old chap,' he told the Ratcatcher, 'but an animal's got to do what an animal's got to do.' He couldn't think of an excuse. There wasn't one, really. He just didn't like work. So these words that he'd heard in some film seemed the best way out of a tricky situation. 'So long,' he said as he climbed in with the friendly lorry driver and curled up next to him on the passenger seat. 'Good riddance,' growled Rufus.

Snowy, it must be said, wasn't exactly as he sounded. His coat, which should have been snow-white, was a dingy grey, mostly because he was too lazy to wash himself. He was also extremely smelly, which was why, although he longed to be a domestic cat, humans refused to allow him in their houses. Since his arrival in Beaumaris, he had, however, secured several human friends and he was a familiar figure at the back doors of the many restaurants and cafes in the town. His disreputable looks, the torn ear and rakish whiskers, seemed to attract sympathy and never a day went by without a dish being placed before him of prime steak, Conwy plaice or custard pie, washed down with a saucer of full cream milk. 'None of that skimmed rubbish for me, if you please,' miaowed Snowy at a cafe owner one day. And she immediately substituted a bowl of thick double cream. 'That's more like it,' he purred. 'You can count on my custom from now on.'

To himself, he repeated his favourite expressions: 'It only costs a little more to travel first class' and 'The best is barely good enough.' They seemed to sum up his whole philosophy, though, of course, he had never paid for anything in his life.

Geraint Growler was as thin and gaunt as Snowy was portly. Somewhere in his ancestry was a streak of Burmese for the fur of Geraint's coat was dark brown in colour and very short. Patches of white and tabby betrayed his other ancestors but he had the golden eyes of the true Burmese and the long, thin tail that tapered to a point. The kink at the end of it twitched when he was angry. His legs were unusually long for any cat.

Susie and Sailor were sister and brother from the same litter. Susie was tabby and Sailor black with a few nautical patches of white. Sailor loved the sea and longed to be a ship's cat; Susie was a landlubber.

Twm Cati was a mischievous black kitten with a spot of white on each cheek which made him look like a clown. He was Scarper's best friend.

Madoc the Magnificent gave a long miaow to bring the meeting to order.

'We are here,' he said, 'to decide how best to deal with the Prickly Problem of Horatio Hedgehog here present.'

He then outlined the problem and told the animals of the evidence they had accumulated so far.

'On a point of order, Mr Chaircat,' said Geraint Growler.

'Yes?' miaowed Madoc.

'This is supposed to be a Council of Cats. But there's a dog present, Miss Kip. I move that said dog should be excluded from our deliberations.'

'Shame on you, Geraint. Miss Kip is our best friend and as such is an Honorary Cat. Motion dismissed,' ordered Madoc. Geraint growled.

'We have to find out how widespread this problem is,' continued Madoc, 'and make sure that if the thieves strike again we get to know of it straight away. We must find out what their motive is, where the hogs are being taken and why.

'To deal with the first part of the problem I suggest we call in our feathered friends, the birds. They have a bird's eye view of the whole country and will be able to tell us quickly whether any similar incidents have taken place, or, indeed, are taking place. We will, of course, have to agree to a Paws Off, Jaws Off treaty for the duration . . . Yes, Geraint, did I hear you growl?'

'You most certainly did. Paws Off, Jaws Off!

Feathered friends! What is the world coming to? You're all going soft in the head. Time was when you could get your teeth into a decent bit of feather and be praised for it. Now we've all got to be palsy-walsies. You wait, we'll be making treaties with rats next. "Nice, kind rats," you'll be telling us, "who are so intelligent, so resourceful. They never meant to bring the Plague or cause disease. It was all the fault of the fleas they carried and they only carried them out of kindness to make sure they had a good square meal." Then you'll be on about poor, maligned fleas. Wrong to scratch them, murder to get them sprayed. There's no end to this rubbish once you start and we cats will end up starving and flea-ridden.'

'I take your point, Geraint Growler,' said Madoc, lashing his tail slowly to keep his cool, 'but we Steel Town Cats are pledged to right wrongs in the animal world. We are detective cats who must use what means we can to find the clues we need to solve crime. And if that means an occasional Paws Off, Jaws Off treaty, so be it.'

'Grrrrrrrrrrrrrrrr,' said Geraint Growler. 'Cats of Steel? Cats of Straw, I say.'

Patchwork rose to his paws. 'I move we support Madoc and go ahead with the Paws Off pact and call in the birds. There's no other way of getting the information we want quickly and we've only got a few days.'

'I second that,' said Esmerelda the Efficient.

'You would,' growled Geraint.

'May I speak?' Elder statescat Marmaduke raised a white-tipped paw.

'Purr,' said Madoc.

'Glancing through the newspaper this morning, I saw something that may be relevant to our case.' Marmaduke Purr was one of the few animals who could both read and write. 'Let me read you the cutting.

A gang which specialises in abducting wild animals is believed to have its headquarters in Manchester. RSPCA officials voiced concern yesterday following an anonymous phone call to their Deansgate office. Said a spokesperson for the Society: 'Hedgehogs are the main victims. We understand the centre of operations is here in the city but we do not know for what purpose the animals are being taken or where they are being held.'

'Good,' said Madoc, 'another lead. One of us will have to go to Manchester to investigate.'

'I will,' barked Miss Kip. 'I have a cousin there, Dartington. He's one of the best runners on the track. Wins hundreds of pounds. He'll help.'

'Right, Miss Kip. On your way as soon as possible. Sort out your own transport and use pigeon post to keep us informed. We'll send reinforcements if and when needed.'

'Bark,' said Kip. She was friendly with all the local train drivers. Getting to the city would be no problem.

'Scarper, go and find Selwyn Starling, Petula Pigeon, Marjorie Jackdaw and Teleri Thrush and tell them I want to see them immediately. Claws off, remember!'

It should be explained at this point, in case you don't know, that all animals understand each other. They speak their own languages. Cats speak miaowpurrese; doggerel is dog language; mice speak squeach and hedgehogs hoggit. But, through a mysterious process known as Espurranto, the sound an individual animal, bird or insect makes is translated so that each can understand the other. To a limited extent, human beings, especially children, can tune into this 'wavelength' if they try hard. Even inanimate objects speak sometimes, though not all that often. The ways of the Great Cat in the Sky are mysterious.

'May I sing my hog song?' squeaked Horatio. 'My spines are feeling distinctly droopy and it would cheer me up no end.'

'Certainly,' said Madoc.

Horatio lifted his head, sniffed the air, and began.

> We are happy hogs and hoglets,
> In the fields we roam so free,
> Thinking only of our supper,
> Breakfast, luncheon and then tea.
>
> Come October we are ready,
> Fat and plump and prickles brisk,
> To seek a nest for winter,
> Snug and warm and free from risk.

Sleep away your cares and worries,
Keep your prickles tightly curled,
Till the sun has warmed the hedgerows
And the worms are sleek as lard.

Baby hoglets, born in springtime,
Eat your fill while summer's here,
For remember pounds are vital
To survive another year.

Keep away from cars and strimmers
And fierce dogs who'll eat you up.
Don't go sniffing things like acid,
Don't eat pellets for the slugs.

Above all, flee the badger,
You can tell him by his smell,
He knows just how to uncurl you
With his claws so long and cruel.

Try and keep your prickles flealess,
It's an awesome task, it's true,
But fleas can bring diseases
That'll be the worse for you.

We are happy hogs and hoglets,
In the fields we roam so free,
Thinking only of our supper,
Breakfast . . .

Horatio's snorts and squeals trailed off as he came to the end of his song and he gave a heart-rending hedgehog sob.

'But we're not happy or free. We're cabined, cribbed, confined. We may even be extinct. Oh, hapless, helpless hogs, oooooh,' he wailed.

'Come now, Horatio. Spines up!' said Madoc briskly. 'Remember you have the Steel Town Cats to help you.'

Chapter Four

Reports were coming in from all over north Wales of vanishing hedgehogs. Sesi Swift had actually witnessed an incident similar to Horatio's as she darted over Blaenau Ffestiniog.

'Why didn't you alight to investigate, you foolish bird?' asked Madoc.

'Swifts don't do that sort of thing, you should know that,' said Sesi as she darted to and fro above the cat's head. 'We're on the wing from the time we leave our nests as chicks until we go to the House of Feathers in the Stratosphere. We do everything in flight, eat, sleep, the lot. Must zoom. Bye-eee!'

Marjorie Jackdaw was next to arrive in a great state of excitement.

'I've found them, I've found them. In Jackdaw City, that's where they are, hundreds of them, all packed up and spikey. Caw, caw, caw!' squawked Marjorie. 'Secret place! On the quay, on the quay! Come and see, come and see!'

'Well done, Marjorie,' miaowed Madoc, 'just give us a few more details . . .'

'Quay-caw, quay-caw, quay-caw,' squawked the excited bird.

'Calm down, my dear,' soothed her friend Petula Pigeon, who had picked up a northern coo during a visit to York. 'You're beginning to sound more like a donkey than a bird. She'll tell you in good time, Madoc, sir. She's all of a tiz at the moment. It's being black that does it: grey is a much calmer colour. No offence, I'm sure,' she added, noting Madoc's fine black coat.

Marjorie was flapping her wings and cawing so loudly it was difficult to grasp what she was saying.

'I've cracked it, I've done it. Claim a reward, claim a reward!' squawked Marjorie. 'Something silver, something shiny for my collection. Want a reward, want a reward!'

'Knowing that you have helped your fellow animals should be reward enough,' said Madoc sternly. 'Now where is this Jackdaw City and what exactly have you seen there?'

'I'll tell you what she told me, if you like,' said Petula Pigeon in her north-country coo. 'I'll act as interpreter, like.'

'If you please, if you please,' cawed Marjorie.

'Jackdaw City is the town of Conwy. There are so many jackdaws there, living in the castle and in cosy crevices on the ancient town walls, that even the human beings who live there are known as "jackdaws". Am I right or am I right, Marjorie, luv?'

'Squawk,' said Marjorie.

'Well, flying over to see her relations, Marjorie just thought she'd pop into the smallest house in England and Wales, the one on the quay, you know.'

Madoc didn't but he twitched his tail and said, 'Continue.'

'It's closed for repairs for a couple of weeks and Marjorie thought she'd have a quick scout round to see if any tourists had dropped any nice rings, keys or coins for her collection.'

'Finders keepers!' squawked Marjorie.

'Unfortunately the hole in the roof wasn't big enough for her to fly through but what she saw fair set her in a tizzy wizzy.'

'There they were,' interrupted Marjorie, 'hundreds and hundreds of hedgehogs, their prickles all sticking out of sacks.'

'Were they alive? Did they say anything?'

'She was that excited she didn't wait,' cooed Petula. 'Just flew straight back to tell you, didn't you, luv?'

'Squawk.'

'Right,' said Madoc. 'Two volunteers to go to Conwy. You, Esmerelda, and you, Scarper.'

'Miaow,' said Scarper.

'I'm afraid, Madoc, it may have escaped your notice but I'm in no condition to make a long journey.'

'Come Esmerelda, it's not like you to refuse the call of duty.'

'Lazy bundle of fleas,' growled Geraint. 'All right bossing other animals around. Another matter when she's told to do something she doesn't fancy. Absolutely typical of grey cats. Wasters, every one.'

'The thing is, Madoc,' said Esmerelda ignoring Geraint's growls, 'I'm going to have kittens.'

'Now there's an excuse!' said Geraint. 'Only a female cat could think up that one. Queens they call 'em and they behave like queens all right. Prima donnas, I'd say. Time was when a cat would have her kittens anywhere and not a day's mousing lost. Kittens, my back paw!'

'All right, Esmerelda, you are excused Jackdaw City,' said Madoc. 'Who is the father?'

'I am,' purred Snowy Tom proudly.

'I suppose you'll be excused duties too,' growled Geraint. 'How about a few days off for friends of the family while we're about it?'

'Silence,' said Madoc, raising an authoritative white paw. 'Snowy and Scarper, go to Conwy! Now!'

'But . . .' began Snowy

'Do you hear? Conwy! Now! Scram! And report back as soon as you can.'

Chapter Five

Miss Kip's cousin Dartington lived in a smart compound with several other racing greyhounds on the outskirts of Manchester. Once a week, sometimes more, they would race at the nearby stadium. Dartington had won thousands of pounds for his owner. When Miss Kip arrived Mr Sheckles could scarcely believe his luck.

'She's a good 'un. We'll run her tonight as a surprise entry,' Mr Sheckles told his assistant, Gary. 'She's a winner or I'll eat my hat.'

Miss Kip very much hoped he wouldn't have to do that since the hat was a wide-brimmed leather affair which she thought would give him terrible indigestion. She happily agreed to run. It wouldn't interfere with her inquiries and what fun it would be.

That night when she was put into her trap on the race track, waiting for the 'off', her heart pounded and her fine white whiskers twitched in anticipation of the chase. Suddenly the trap lifted and there, racing ahead, was the hare, a mechanical one in fact, but just as much fun to pursue.

She ran like the wind, a golden streak along the stadium floor. Ahead were two other hounds, Miss Rosie and Miss Pimms. She must catch them up, she must beat them. She had never known competition before and she savoured the exhilaration of it. Her powerful lungs filled up and her breath came in steady pants. She stretched her long golden legs to take bigger strides. Soon she was a nose, a head, a length in front. The bright lights that lit the arena burned down on her back and the crowd roared 'Miss Kip, Miss Kip!' Victory was in sight.

Then she heard thundering paws coming up behind her. 'Pol-ly, Pol-ly' roared the crowd. She was the favourite and was well known for making a quick spurt at the end. 'Pol-ly, Pol-ly.'

Miss Kip redoubled her efforts, thrust her black nose forward and ran as she'd never run before.

'She's won, Miss Kip's won! We're millionaires! Wonderful! What an animal! We'll take her to White City in London, she'll sweep the board.'

Mr Sheckles was, as he told the Press, 'over the moon'. Miss Kip was so thrilled by her success she didn't heed the warning signs.

'You realise that if you're too good he'll want to keep you,' warned cousin Dartington. 'You may never return to Anglesey.'

'But this is my life now. I'm a winner, I'm a star,' barked Miss Kip. 'Why should I want to go back to boring little Anglesey? Manchester today, London tomorrow, and who knows where after that.'

'We know where all right,' growled Dartington's friend, Demon. 'Simon and Snip went the other night. Too old at four, Mr Sheckles reckoned. That gives me another year and you, Miss Kip, no more than two.'

'Went where?' barked Miss Kip. 'I'll go anywhere.'

'Where, indeed? I could say a lot but it wouldn't do,' growled Demon darkly.

'Quiet, Demon,' said Dartington. 'You know it's forbidden to mention "After Racing". Live for the Day, that's our motto here.'

'Live for the Day,' barked Miss Kip.

The next time out she won again, and the next and the next. Her name was in the newspapers, she was interviewed on television, publishers offered six-figure advances for her life story. Miss Kip T-shirts were already on sale; Miss Kip mugs were in

Miss Kip wins again!

production in the Staffordshire potteries. A Hollywood producer was negotiating film rights and a pet food company wanted to use her name to endorse its latest product.

Life was a helter-skelter, the attention of the media intoxicating.

'Miss Kip,' barked Dartington that night. 'I've heard something about those hedgehogs you mentioned when you first arrived. It seems there's an organisation in the city called Just Ask. They'll undertake to do anything for a price and one of the things they've been "just asked" to do is collect hedgehogs. They've got to have a consignment of 500 ready by the 31st.'

'The 31st,' said Miss Kip. 'That's the date Horatio heard mentioned. Well, it's the 26th now. Plenty of time.'

'It's not plenty of time at all,' said Dartington. 'You must tell Madoc.'

'Must?' barked Miss Kip. 'I don't have to do anything, not now I'm a star. Once I've pad-marked my Hollywood contract then I'll think about it, if I choose.'

'Kip, listen to me. A racing life is a short life. When you're past your peak, and that won't be long, you'll either be put down or thrown out . . .'

'What do you mean, put down?'

'Exterminated, killed, probably with a lethal injection, possibly shot.'

'Rubbish.'

'What do you think Demon meant when he talked about Simon and Snip?'

'That they'd gone to a luxury rest home, of course. Somewhere smart where only the best hounds go.'

'No, Kip, that's not what he meant at all. The truth is – and don't growl when I'm talking to you – the truth is that when we're finished here we're put to sleep, or shot dead or thrown out to fend for ourselves. No food, no shelter, no home. The best we can hope for is to be picked up by some kindly human and taken to a Greyhound Rescue Centre. That's why we never talk about A.R., After Racing. It's strictly forbidden, as I told Demon.

'No one, but no one, must mention A.R. I only do it now for your sake. We racers here, we understand the situation and we accept it. We've no other life. We live for the day. Burying our noses in the sand, some might say, but that's the way it is.

'I'm breaking the rules to talk to you like this because, although you're my cousin, you're different. You have a home, people in Anglesey who love you, friends like Madoc the Magnificent who rely on you. Don't throw it all away for a few days of glory.'

'I'm a star,' barked Kip.

'There's another fate, worse than instant death, that we dare not even hint at it is so horrible,' continued Dartington, 'but I'll tell you about it to try and bring you to your senses. Those hounds that are not put down or released into the wild are crated up and sent, squashed together and starving, to race in

49

Spain. It's very hot there and the hounds live in appalling conditions, caged for 23 hours a day. They are made to race on rough tracks until they die, literally in harness. Their skins are used to make cheap leather goods for the tourist trade. And those that don't die on the track, dogs who are not fast enough or ones who have broken their legs, for instance, they are sent for vivisection, medical experiments on live animals. Do you understand what I'm saying? Go back to Anglesey before it is too late.'

'I'm a star,' barked Miss Kip.

Chapter Six

Scarper and Snowy Tom arrived in Jackdaw City. It was evening and the cries of nesting jackdaws, and of seagulls having a last foray on the quay before settling down for the night, were over-whelming. The two cats flattened their ears to deaden the sound.

'Here's a comfortable looking hostelry,' said Snowy Tom, pointing his whiskers towards an ancient harbour-side inn. 'Supper time, I would say. I'll just slip in for a quick half pie while you do a recce. I'd ask you to join me but you're too young for such places.'

Left alone, Scarper ran up on to the walls that encircle the town in the shape of a harp. Built at the same time as Conwy Castle, in 1283, they stand high above the town and from them Scarper could see over the tops of the houses. There, on the quay, was the roof he wanted, the roof of the smallest house in Wales and England.

He jumped from the wall to a roof, scampered along the tiles to another roof and eventually reached the one in question. Sure enough, there was the hole Marjorie Jackdaw had mentioned. He began scratching away at the crumbling fabric to make an opening wide enough for him first to see, and then to crawl, through.

There was a bed in the tiny room, once occupied, amazingly, by a man over six feet tall, and on it was a linen sack out of which hundreds and thousands of prickles protruded.

'Hogs, are you alive? I'm Scarper Purr Kitten and I've come to save you.'

'Swwwwish . . .'

What an odd noise, thought Scarper. It didn't sound like an animal at all, let alone a hedgehog.

'I'm coming down and I'll get you out of there in no time. You'll have bugs galore to eat before you can say "Fleas" or my fur's not ginger.'

'Uuuuuuuuuugh.'

Another strange sound. Scarper had heard nothing like it in his life before.

'Don't insult us with words like "bugs" and "fleas". Who's going to want us with bugs? We'll be thrown on the scrapheap. Rejects!'

The voice was difficult to understand and was accompanied by a swishing sound. Scarper could only just make out what it said. He decided that close confinement had affected their brains and that these hedgehogs were stupider than most.

'All right, I'll release you because that's what Madoc the Magnificent wants me to do but I think you're rude and ungrateful. Growl.'

So saying, Scarper jumped down onto the bed and began tearing at the sack with his claws.

'Mind my handle! Mind my soft rubber cushioning! I'll never grace a lady's dressing table after this! No salon will look at me with damaged bristles! Ouch!'

'You miserable bunch of moaning prickles,' growled Scarper. 'This is the last time I rescue hedgeho . . .' He stopped in amazement and gave a loud 'Mrrrrrow', for emerging from the sack, instead of hedgehogs, were hundreds and hundreds of hairbrushes.

'But . . . How . . .?' began Scarper. 'I thought you were hedgehogs.'

'What a disgusting thought! Dirty, smelly, flea-ridden hedgehogs! No, we're smart, expensive hairbrushes, destined for the top hairdressing salons in the country. We were on our way to London, from Birmingham, our place of manufacture, when our van was raided and we were stolen and brought here to this stuffy little house.'

'It's a very nice house,' protested Scarper. 'It's got everything an animal could want, comfortable chairs, a warm stove – and a few promising looking mouseholes.'

'Exactly. An animal. But we are nothing so lowly as animal. We're more your vegetable and mineral. Made to the highest specifications. Designed to brush only the most aristocratic of hair.'

'But I thought bristles came from pigs and you're all bristle.'

'Do you mind?' said the superior hairbrush, who appeared to be spokesbrush for them all. 'Pigs' bristles are a thing of the past. We're your modern hairbrush, simulated bristle, man-made fibre, so much more refined, you know.'

'Yes, you do seem very refined,' said Scarper, who hadn't met many refined animals let alone hairbrushes. 'But how can you speak? I thought only animals and humans and insects could make noises that meant something. I mean, you haven't even got mouths.'

'Ignorant, arrogant animal,' said the spokesbrush. 'All sorts of things that haven't got mouths can speak. What about the wind and the sea and the clouds when they clash in thunder? They haven't got mouths but don't tell me, you foolish kitten, that they don't make meaningful noises.

'Pretty well everything can say something, or, indeed, sing something, if the time and place are opportune. It's just that most of the time we don't choose to. It's a faculty we can do without. It wouldn't, you see, normally speaking, increase our usefulness, would it? What would anyone want with a talking hairbrush?'

'Well,' began Scarper, at a loss for miaows. If this

54

loquacious brush was anything to go by, he, for one, wouldn't want it brushing his fur. 'Well, I . . .'

At that moment he heard a noise downstairs. The key was in the lock, someone was trying to get in.

'Blisters!' said a man's voice. 'The wrong key. Go and get the other lot from the car, Gwil, while I wait here and take a breather.'

'Right-ho!' said Gwilym.

'Quick,' said Scarper, 'we must scarper. 'I'll take you in my mouth and throw you up one by one to that hole in the ceiling and then you must make your way over the rooftops to safety. I'll follow.'

'Prepare to be thrown!' said the spokesbrush.

Scarper had just got down to the last five brushes when he heard the key turn in the lock. Tossing mice was one thing; propelling over one hundred hairbrushes several feet in the air was quite another. The muscles in his neck and back ached from the task.

A red face appeared in the hole at the top of the stair well. The mouth in the face dropped open when the eyes saw Scarper and, with the blast of astonished breath that emerged from the gawping orifice, came the overpowering smell . . . of garlic.

'What a funny smell,' thought Scarper, but never having sniffed garlic before, he didn't connect it with Horatio's evidence. With enormous effort, he hurled the last hairbrush skywards and prepared to jump himself. As he did so, a rough hand grasped his leg, the one with the white garter of fur, and he was dragged from the bed.

'Look what we 'ave 'ere. A kitten, a nasty thieving, ginger kitten. Caught 'im red-pawed throwing our nice 'airbrushes to the four winds. What you done that for, then? Speak up.'

'Grrrrr,' said Scarper.

'Careful, Alf, he may bite you,' came a Welsh voice from below stairs.

'Bite me? I'll not give 'im the chance, bad tempered, flea-ridden moggie,' said Alf. 'Them's cost us, you know, me and Gwil. Nice bit-a lolly we 'ad tied up there and now we lost it, ain't we? All because of some interfering marmalade mouse chaser. What d'you say, Gwil, we do with 'im? Drown 'im? String 'im up? Pull 'is claws out?'

Scarper struggled but Alf had him by the scruff of his neck.

Fortunately, the smallest house in Wales and England also possesses the smallest and narrowest of staircases and Alf's feet were among the largest in the UK. He missed his footing, let go of Scarper and crashed onto the floor below, knocking Gwilym into the metal cooker. The swearing that followed in both languages is not repeatable.

Scarper gripped the top of the stairs, pulled himself up, jumped onto the bed and from there leapt to the hole in the ceiling. He was free.

'Let's get out of this doll's house before I get catophobia,' said Alf when he'd finished cursing.

'Claustrophobia,' corrected Gwilym.

56

Snowy Tom had a fine welcome at the Liverpool Arms. The landlady, distressed by his shabby appearance but impressed by the deep, earthquake-like rumble of his purr, gave him the remains of that day's 'special', steak and kidney pie. He had refused chips ('my weight, you understand') but thought he just might manage a small saucer of vanilla icecream. 'Not too small,' he miaowed as the landlady moved away and began to close the carton. He purred as another spoonful was dished up.

'I could move in here,' thought Snowy. 'Suit me down to the tip of my bushy tail. Scarper's a big kitten now. He can manage those hogs perfectly well without my help, I'm sure. And Esmerelda and the kittens? Well, kittens need a mother but they don't need me. Even Esmerelda will probably growl at me once she has the kittens, thinking I'm going to eat them or something equally barmy. And Madoc? He's always so active and enthusiastic, always looking for a problem to solve, a project to start on, a wrong to right. But me, I like the leisured life, time to sit and stare, and a nice, comfortable place like this where I can contemplate and watch the world go by, bothering nobody . . .'

Snowy finished his second helping of icecream, stretched himself and set off towards a corner seat by the window.

'Poor homeless animal,' said the landlady. 'Have a nice sleep and then we'll see what we can do about cleaning you up. You are a bit smelly and I have to think of my customers.'

'A pint of bitter and two shandies, please,' a man's voice said.

'Right away,' said the landlady. 'Now be a good cat,' she told Snowy, 'and I'll see you in half an hour when we're not so busy. We'll put you in a nice bath and we'll soon have you whiter than white.'

Whiter than white? No, it was just not on. Perhaps she did make the best steak and kidney pies in north Wales but he, Snowy Tom, was not to be bought. He would leave in precisely twenty minutes after a short catnap. Oh, the softness of the windowseat cushion! Oh, the warmth of the evening sun! He purred, but he kept a wary half-open eye on the door.

In twenty minutes precisely he was off.

Outside, an extraordinary sight met his eyes. Hundreds of hairbrushes were marching along the quay; past the pub, the yachts at their moorings, the aquarium and the chandler's shop; past the fish stall and the harbour master's office and on over the bridge that spans the wide Conwy estuary. At the roundabout they turned right and headed for the motorway. And as they marched they sang this song:

Harris, Hengist, Humph and Hal,
Helen, Haf and Hubert,
Hereward and Hippolyte,
Harriet, Huw and Humbert.

Who are we who sing so loud,
Heads high in the air?
The answer is a simple one,
We're brushes for your hair.

On handle-tip we hop along,
Bristles boldly forward,
Hester, Horace, Hilda, Ham,
Hedda, Hope and Howard.

Our story is that we were wronged,
Stolen from our factory,
Now we're marching back to show
We're willing workers – actually.

Our boss will sell us round the world,
Expensive items we,
We brush your hair like nothing else,
Just try us and you'll see.

But never mention, if you please,
For hogs we were mistook,
For hogs are famous for their fleas,
And fleas we cannot brook.

So hop your way to Birmingham,
Hazel, Hank and Harper,
Keep well to the side of the busy road
And sing your thanks to Scarper!

Snowy Tom looked on in amazement. He sat down and turned his head to give the fur on his back a quick lick. If the vision was still there when he looked again, then it was real. If not, he was having halucinations. Something in that steak pie, no doubt. He finished licking – and the hairbrushes were still there, still marching, still singing. And on the quay, a little further on, sat a small ginger kitten, waving a white-tipped paw.

'Scarper Purr Kitten, what is happening?' said Snowy, trotting up as fast as an overweight animal can to the younger cat. 'I'm a very confused cat.'

'Don't worry, Snowy,' said Scarper. 'It's all sorted out. They were hairbrushes.'

'I can see that,' said Snowy. 'I'm not stupid. But what about the hedgehogs?'

'They were hairbrushes.'

'I know they were hairbrushes. I've been standing here looking at them too, you know. I thought at first I'd been drugged by that landlady with an obsession for cleanliness and I was seeing things. No, what I want to know is what happened to the hogs?'

'They were hairbrushes,' repeated Scarper.

Poor kitten, thought Snowy, he's obviously taken leave of his senses. What will his Great Uncle Marmaduke say?

'Scarper,' said Snowy, 'I know singing hairbrushes are hard for an animal to accept but in my long life I've seen many strange sights and, as long as they don't want to hurt you or steal your food, why worry?

Singing hairbrushes are not a problem. It's not worth a second of one of your nine lives. Calm down, lick your fur, compose yourself and we'll try once more to tackle the problem of the imprisoned hedgehogs.'

'But I have solved the problem, Snowy,' mewed Scarper crossly. 'Don't you see, those hedgehogs I went to rescue turned out to be hairbrushes, so I rescued them instead.' Was Snowy going funny in the head in his old age, he wondered? Then he let out an anguished: 'Mrrrrrrrooooow . . .'

A tall male human had stolen up behind him and grabbed him by the tail.

'Got yer this time, you nasty bit of ginger fluff, and this time yer gonna pay for your thieving ways. I'll throw you to the eels in the river, that's what I'll do. They like a bit of plump kitten, eh, Gwil?'

'No Alf, be fair, *chwarae teg*, it's not a capital offence he's committed and we would have had terrible problems, anyway, getting rid of those brushes. Besides, they say it's bad luck to kill a cat, especially in Conwy. Put him in this empty sack and throw him out on the motorway. That way it's not us that's responsible for his decease, see?'

Gwilym didn't really know if killing cats in Conwy was especially unlucky but he had a soft spot for the feline species and wanted to give Scarper a chance. What he did know was that Alf was plagued by superstition. He wouldn't risk harming Scarper if he thought it would bring him bad luck.

'Very well, Gwil, you win,' said Alf, and threw

Scarper into the proferred sack. 'You can count this as one of your nine lives lost, mog. Now let's go have a jar.'

Snowy, who had run out of the way, was alarmed to see the two men enter the hostelry he had so recently vacated. Even at the risk of a bath he would have to follow.

They sat down with two foaming pints at a table by the fireplace. It must be lovely and snug in winter, thought Snowy, with the fire blazing and logs crackling. An animal could be comfortable here . . .

But water, soapy water, a bath! What an indignity! He laid his ears back, flush with the matted fur on his head, and snarled a silent snarl. He ran behind the log basket and crouched low so he could keep an eye on the sack that contained the hapless Scarper.

After a few gulps of their beer the men began to relax.

'You can't win 'em all,' said Alf philosophically. 'We might have made a packet on them hairbrushes but, there again, we might not.'

'No indeed,' said Gwilym.

'Distribution could have been tricky and return on investment would be low.'

'What investment? We didn't pay for them.'

'Of course we didn't. Investment in time and thought, I mean. Time's money, you know. Brains is money too.'

'No chance of you being a millionaire then,' muttered Gwilym under his breath.

'Anyway, we'll do better with those other prickly things,' continued Alf, who didn't seem to have heard Gwilym's remark. 'The money's as good as guaranteed there.'

'Yes indeed,' said Gwilym. 'And foreign money too. American dollars. As safe as houses, that.'

Snowy, and Scarper in his sack, strained their ears. Prickly things? Surely they hadn't stumbled on the hedgehog thieves after all? Snowy's nose twitched. He smelt the unmistakable smell of garlic. Wasn't that one of Horatio's clues, a man who smelt of garlic? Alf continued:

'The 31st, remember. That's the day we've got to get them all ready for the off and that's the day we get the lolly. A nice present for me birthdai, eh Gwil?'

Of course. Those were the very words Horatio Hedgehog had heard when his colony was hognapped! And spoken with that London accent, so strange to Welsh hogs' ears: 'The 31st, me birthdai!'

'Yes indeed,' said Gwilym.

'We've got hundreds of the horrible creatures now, nasty snuffling things. Can't think why they want them in America.'

'Because they haven't got any of their own, that's why,' said Gwilym.

'And better off without them, I'd say. But ours not to reason why, eh, Gwil?'

'Yes indeed.'

'If our boss at Just Ask just asks and the money's right, we do as we're told, no questions, eh?'

'Yes indeed,' said Gwilym. 'But I wonder what will happen to the hogs when they get to the United States? Will they settle down, do you think? Will they be happy?'

'Will they settle down? Will they be happy?' echoed Alf, imitating Gwilym's north Wales accent. 'What are you? Some kind of animal social worker? No, they don't settle down, they die because they don't like the climate, but that's not our problem, is it?'

'Then that's not fair on the customers either,' Gwilym protested.

'Blisters to the customers. They knows when they buys 'em they probably won't survive. They takes a chance, don't they? All we've got to do is make sure we've got 500 of the prickly pests crated up and ready for transportation by the 31st. And the lolly in crisp dollar notes in our pockets.'

Snowy and Scarper shivered as they heard these callous words. They remembered what Horatio's Uncle Hywel had said about selling hogs to humans in a hogless land. It seemed the wise old hog had hit the nail on the head. They must get back to Madoc and report their findings. But where would the hogs be on the 31st? Where was transportation point?

'What happens if they die on the flight?' asked Gwilym. 'I don't suppose they are used to flying.'

'I don't suppose they are but that's not our problem either,' said Alf. 'Once we hand them over and take our money, that's it. Finish.'

So the hogs would be taken to an airport. Which

airport? Snowy and Scarper hoped they would remember all these details to tell Madoc. Cats have good memories but they're not as good as those of elephants, who, of course, never forget anything.

'But what happens if we're stopped, if anyone looks in the crates?' Gwilym persisted.

'What, in a remote spot like that? Do me a favour!'

'And what about that law that says you mustn't be cruel to wild animals?'

'I've not been cruel. I've picked them up and I've put them in a crate. What's so cruel about that? My conscience is clear. Come on, drink up and let's be on our way.'

Snowy and Scarper realised they must act quickly. They had communicated with each other by cat telepathy and they knew exactly what to do.

By good luck, Scarper had been placed in the same sack that had been used to store the hairbrushes, the sack that, thanks to his earlier endeavours, already had a substantial hole in it. All he had to do was make the hole a bit wider and he would be free. It was work of a moment for a sharp-toothed kitten.

Snowy signalled to Scarper that he would create a diversion. His plan had a double purpose and he hoped he could complete it before the two men became aware of what was happening.

It was a warm evening and the pub door stood open. The landlady was busy with her pies: her husband had taken over at the bar. Snowy got up, streched himself and strolled over to the table where

65

the two men were sitting. He put his bottom against one of the four trouser legs on view, raised his tail and started to spray. He then moved to a trouser leg from the second pair and repeated the performance. It was the sort of spraying that only tom cats can do. Normally the purpose is to mark territory and attract a mate. The scent is exceptionally pungent. Once on furniture or clothing it is very difficult, if not impossible, to get rid of.

This time Snowy didn't want territory or a mate: he wanted to imprint his scent on these two villains so he could track them down again. Alf might stop eating garlic but he'd never get cat scent off his trousers. As he sprayed, Snowy's tail quivered. His face bore an expression of intense concentration.

'Funny smell this beer has,' said Alf. 'Welsh, I suppose. Nothing's any good north of Watford in my opinion.'

'*Chwarae teg*, Alf, be fair,' protested Gwilym, 'it's the best . . .' His voice trailed off as the smell, something like overripe melons, hit his nostrils. '*Ofnadwy*, disgusting, horrible! A dirty, stinking tom cat!' he yelled, seeing Snowy running off towards the open door.

'Look out, that ginger thing's escaping!' yelled Alf. 'Stop thief! Grab his tail, you idiot!'

It was too late. The cats had scarpered.

'My fur and whiskers!' said Snowy as they sat with the engine driver on the train taking them back to Anglesey, 'we've had some narrow escapes today.'

'I have, you mean,' mewed Scarper. 'All you've done is stuff yourself full of pies and ice-cream as far as I can tell.'

'You impertinent kitten!' said Snowy, and cuffed him with his paw. 'I nearly suffered one of the worst fates an animal can endure.'

'And what's that, pray?' miaowed Scarper.

'A bath,' said Snowy, 'a soapy bath.'

Chapter Seven

Back in Beaumaris, Madoc listened with attention to Snowy and Scarper's account of what they had seen and heard in Conwy.

'It all tallies with the information I have received from Manchester,' he growled. 'Let us recap. We know the name of the organisation, Just Ask, and we know where its headquarters are: Manchester. We have positively identified the two main villains, Alf and Gwilym. We know why Horatio's friends have been hognapped and we know which country they are destined for.

'We know, too, that they will be transported from this country by aeroplane and we know the date of the flight. What we don't know is the location of the airport.'

'It's remote,' mewed Scarper, 'so it can't be Liverpool or Manchester or London.'

'Right, Scarper. Let us make further deductions from the information in paw. Reports indicate that the villains are working in this area so the chances are it will be an airport, or airstrip, somewhere near here,' added Madoc, lashing his tail as he spoke. It is a well known fact that slow and steady lashing of the tail concentrates the mind wonderfully.

'So what's our next move?' asked Snowy.

'Our next move,' said Madoc in slow and

deliberate purrs, 'is to contact Harry the Hawk. He has a wide domain and a sharp eye. He'll know exactly where the airstrips are and if any funny business is going on. Snowy and Scarper, you'll have to go and see him. Geraint Growler and I have other business to attend to.'

'What's that?' growled Geraint.

'Go to Manchester and find out more about Just Ask and, most important of all, bring Miss Kip home. I have had disturbing news from her cousin Dartington. It seems her head's been turned by the bright city lights and the excitement of the race track. If I don't get to her soon her racing career will be over and she'll be packed off for vivisection or sent to run till she drops on the rough tracks in Spain. Dartington's told me everything.'

The animals shuddered. Vivisection was a word seldom mentioned in animal circles. Madoc had lowered his voice to a soft growl even to utter it.

Geraint was fond of Miss Kip but he couldn't see the necessity of going to Manchester.

'Can't we use those mongrels who run messages for us on the Catmail? Surely we don't actually have to go there?'

'You mustn't use the word "mongrels" any more, Geraint,' Madoc rebuked him. 'It's not politically correct. They have to be called "pedigree mix" now.'

'Ridiculous,' growled Geraint. 'Pedigree mix sounds more like a biscuit. Anyway, why should we ape human beings? We're sensible animals. What's

70

the world coming to when you can't call a moggie a moggie?'

'That,' said Madoc, 'is not in dispute. But I am in charge here, Geraint, and you're coming with me to Manchester.' Under his breath Geraint grumbled that it seemed they were not all so equal when it came to giving commands. Out loud he growled, 'Oh, all right.'

'May I come too?' squealed Horatio Hedgehog, who had been following the conversation from underneath a pile of mown grass. 'There must be lots of good gardens there where I could find a slug or two.'

'Don't you ever think of anything but your stomach?' growled Geraint Growler. 'You're worse than Snowy Tom. Do we have to take him with us, Madoc? He's a right misery. And now he's got us cats into trouble by stealing and eating a chicken.'

'Is that right, Horatio?' asked Madoc.

'Well, it's like this,' said Horatio. 'The season started chilly and now it's turned uncommon hot and the earth's gone hard and, oooohhh, the heat, I've come over quite faint.'

'Excuses, excuses,' growled Geraint.

'But why steal a chicken just because it's hot?' asked Madoc.

'As you know, there's been no rain for some time and the ground's got terribly hard. It's more than a poor hog can do to dig for grubs. And grubs is life to us. A hog must eat.'

'Does precious little else as far as I can see,' grumbled Geraint.

'I see your problem, Horatio, and I'll try and beg some cat food for you off our human friends. But no more chickens. It's vital for us animals to stay on the right side of humans. Once humans turns nasty, they can be very nasty. And powerful. Remember that. It's part of the Animal Code.'

'Sorry, Madoc,' squealed Horatio. 'But can I come too?'

'No, you stay here with Patchwork and Marmaduke and wait for hog news. A big city is no place for a hedgehog. We're streetwise from our Steel Town days and can run fast and dodge through traffic but you'd be a squashed hog in no time.'

'And us, Madoc, where do we find Harry the Hawk?' miaowed Snowy.

'He has a stately eyrie in a place called Plas Newydd, just up the Strait from here near Llanfairpwll. The bus will drop you off there after it's taken us to the station. I've fixed it with the driver. He's a good friend of mine. We'll do some ratting for him in return when all this business is over.' It was a good arrangement Madoc had with many humans and it worked to their mutual interest.

'Plas Newydd?' mewed Scarper. 'Isn't that a big place, a sort of estate where pheasants live?' He licked his lips at the thought of a tasty morsel.

'Yes, but don't put paw on pheasant or the gamekeepers will have you,' warned Madoc. 'Even

Harry the Hawk doesn't attack his own pheasants. You'll probably find him in the rhododendron garden, perched on top of a Scots pine. Give him a loud caterwaul and say I sent you.'

'Miaow,' said the two cats.

'Right, shake a paw,' said Madoc the Magnificent. 'we must be off in ten minutes.'

'May I just go and look at my kittens before we leave?' asked Snowy. 'I gather there's been a happy event since we've been away.'

'Purr, by all means,' said Madoc.

Snowy found Esmerelda lying in a soft bed in the corner of a garden shed. Tessa, the twelve-year-old in Miss Kip's human family, had made it for her. It was the last thing she did before falling ill. She had put a curtain over the window to protect the new-born kittens' eyes from the light and at first even Snowy found it difficult to make out what was happening. But he heard mewing, and as the pupils of his eyes enlarged in the darkness, he saw, snuggled up to Esmerelda, four tiny bundles of glorious fur, four beautiful kittens.

'It's me, Snowy Tom,' he said. 'Are they like me? Are they good looking like me? Let me see.'

'Grrrrrrrr,' said Esmerelda.

'Come off it, Es,' said Snowy, 'Madoc's sending me off to Llanfairpwll and I don't know when I'll be back. I'd like to get just a peep at my kittens before I go.'

'My grrrrrrrr kittens,' growled Esmerelda, and hissed horribly, but she did move away enough to let Snowy get a glimpse. There were two males, one snow-white and one black and white, and two females, a tortoiseshell and a grey. The grey had a small black splodge over her left eye in the shape of a question mark, just like her mother. Their eyes were still closed, their ears were small and stubby and their tails stuck out like mice tails. They were extremely hungry.

Snowy purred with fatherly pride. 'My, I mean, our kittens,' he purred. 'The best kittens in the whole world!'

'Purr,' said Esmerelda, and then remembered that she should be growling just in case Snowy became jealous and attacked her offspring. It happened in the animal world. 'Prrr, grrr,' she said, and drew the kittens to her.

Chapter Eight

Madoc the Magnificent and Geraint Growler caught the train at Llanfairpwllgwyngyllgogerychwyrn-drobwll-llantysiliogogogoch. Fortunately it was a through train to Manchester Piccadilly and, since they knew the driver, they didn't have to pay.

'Just come and do some mousing for me one night,' said Alun, who lived near the station. 'I've had quite a problem with mice lately and they frighten my little girl.'

It seemed a long way to the cats: Llanfairfechan, Penmaenmawr, Llandudno Junction, Colwyn Bay, Rhyl, Prestatyn, Flint, Shotton . . .

'Look, Madoc,' miaowed Geraint with excitement, 'Shotton, our Steel Town where it all started.'

Madoc remembered with pride the days when he had rallied redundant cats from Shotton, and indeed from all over the country, to march on London to see the prime minister. He had succeeded that time in getting work for his fellow mousers. Now he must save Horatio's friends. And Miss Kip.

The train continued: Chester, Runcorn, Warrington Bank Quay, Eccles, Manchester Oxford Road, Manchester Piccadilly.

'Here you are,' said Alun. 'Be careful how you go in the big city and be back here in good time if you want a return ride.'

'Purr,' said Madoc

The two cats ran the length of the platform, darting through passengers' legs. They emerged into hazy sunlight, the smell of car exhausts and a rumble of traffic that took them by surprise after the quiet of Anglesey.

'First we'll go to the offices of Just Ask and see if we can pick up any more information,' miaowed Madoc, 'and then we'll go to the greyhound stadium and find Miss Kip. Petula Pigeon flew over the other day and did a recce – she knows about towns – and she has given me exact instructions. Come on! This way!'

The city pavements were hot on their paws. Alley cats gave them dirty looks as they passed.

'Scruffy country mousers, don't come trespawsing on our patch!' they growled menancingly.

'Flea-ridden townies!' jeered Geraint. 'Dustbin raiders! Garbage scavengers!'

'Cut it out, Geraint. Ignore them. We've got work to do,' said Madoc sternly.

The premises of Just Ask were on the fifteenth floor of a twenty-storey office block. The cats waited for a human to open the lift and then crouched in the corner of the cubicle hoping no one would throw them out.

Nobody did. In fact the occupants of the lift took not the slightest notice of them. They were all too busy riffling through files and briefcases, and arranging meetings, conferences and presentations on their mobile phones. Not for the first time, Madoc wondered why humans made such a fuss about their work. He supposed it was because they were all terrified of losing their jobs. Yes, that must be it. He knew from his own experience how harsh that could be. Security ripped from under your paws at a stroke and growing kittens at home to feed. No wonder these humans looked so worried.

No one was going to the fifteenth floor so Madoc jumped up and pressed the button with his paw. The lift lurched upwards and once again the two cats felt as if they were leaving half their stomachs behind. 'Oh, my fur and heaving whiskers,' moaned Geraint.

'Best paw forward,' said Madoc as the lift door opened.

Just Ask occupied an open-plan office in which three people were at work: Mr Fixit, the boss, and two assistants, Doris and Robert. The cats ran to a corner and crouched on the floor, gazing intently at a small hole in the skirting board as if on an important mousing mission.

'What gives with them animals, eh?' asked Mr Fixit.

'Vermin control,' said Doris. She had learnt that with Mr Fixit any answer was better than none at all.

The telephone rang. Mr Fixit pressed a button on a panel on his desk. 'Fixit here,' he said.

The caller's voice came out of a speaker in the same panel. Mr Fixit couldn't be bothered with telephones you have to hold. The conversation could therefore be heard by everyone; the cats were in luck.

'Alf here,' the voice said. 'Me and Gwilym's got what you wanted, 500 of them prickly things, all in pens and ready for crating up. When do we get the lolly?'

'Not so fast, my friend,' said Mr Fixit, 'I'm the one who's fixed the deal. I get the money in American dollars and then pay you your whack, you and Gwilym both.'

'So you'll be there at the airfield when we hand over the consignment, like?'

''Course I will. You don't think I'd trust you two with all that dough, do you? It'll only take me about two hours down the Expressway. I'll be there, six o'clock in the morning, pronto! Mind you're not late. Welsh hogs, are they?'

''As'right,' said Alf. 'They seem the fattest and best. Something to do with Llanys-something-or-other beetles, or so Gwilym says.'

'OK, OK, don't bother me with long words. Good work, boys. Now, don't forget, bring a flask of coffee and some bacon butties with you. I'll be wanting breakfast and so will the pilot. There's a small reception room where we can eat, nice and comfy like, after we've loaded them hogs.'

'You're on, boss,' said Alf.

Madoc and Geraint had the information they wanted. They could tell, from Mr Fixit's route and timing, that the airfield to be used was definitely in their part of Wales. They knew, too, that there would be a break for breakfast in an airport reception room, valuable minutes in which to plot a rescue. It was time to go.

'Don't think I've forgotten your stupidity with the hairbrushes,' Mr Fixit continued in sterner tones. 'How could you possibly lose that number of brushes?'

'It was that ginger kitten that done it,' complained Alf, 'egged on by a smelly, dirty-white tom cat. He made us stink and all, me and Gwil. Put 'is nasty scent all over our trouser legs and we ain't got no change of clothes with us neither, ain't us?'

'Cats, did you say?' said Mr Fixit. 'There are two cats here, one a great black thing with a white front and the other sort of brown. Just come in and sat sitting cool as you please.'

'A big black and white one!' Alf's voice was hoarse.

'Yes.'

'With whopping great whiskers?'

'Yes.'

'It's him, it's their leader, I've heard all about him. He's dangerous, that one. Nab 'im.'

Madoc and Geraint ran towards the open door.

'Stop them cats! Stop thieves!' cried Mr Fixit, and pressed the security button to summon aid.

'You're trapped now,' he called after the retreating cats. 'That button I've pressed stops all the lifts and locks the doors. Prepare to end the last of your nine lives.'

'Let's try the stairs,' miaowed Madoc. 'Here! There must be some way out.'

They almost fell down the stairs in their hurry to get away, closely pursued by Mr Fixit, Doris and Robert.

There were landings where the staircase turned and on each landing was a window. They were of the type that tilted open just a few inches. Enough to let a cat through, thought Madoc, but not a human being.

'We'll have to squeeze through a window,' said Madoc. 'It's our only way. There's bound to be something out there we can hold on to until the coast is clear.'

They prepared to jump for the small aperture. And then they saw a face, a human face outside the window. A face with bright blue eyes and a ginger moustache, topped by a flat cloth cap.

'Hey, cats, can I be of help?' asked the man, who appeared to be swinging in some sort of cradle. In his right hand he carried a long, flat object on a handle, to which was attached a sponge. He was a window cleaner.

'You first, Geraint,' said Madoc. 'I'll stay behind to ward off any trouble.'

'But I don't like heights . . .' Geraint began.

'Jump!' ordered Madoc the Magnificent.

Geraint obeyed and soon he was safe outside in the cradle. Madoc crouched low in the jumping position and prepared to follow. He got a grip on the window ledge outside with his front paws and began to pull himself through. But he was a much bigger cat than Geraint; his body stuck fast.

'That's the ringleader, grab him!' ordered Mr Fixit. Doris and Robert started to tug at Madoc's lower half but they hadn't reckoned with the sharp claws of his back paws.

'Ouch, he's ripped my hand,' cried Robert, staggering back with blood dripping from his right hand.

'Ow, he's torn my new blouse,' whined Doris. 'That's enough. Catching cats is against Union rules. This wasn't in our job description.'

'Give over,' said Mr Fixit, 'I'll sort him out. I'll cut his tail off, that'll learn him.'

Mr Fixit took a penknife from his pocket and began to pull out the blade. It only took a few seconds but it was enough time to allow the window cleaner to force the window open a fraction more. Madoc pulled himself through just as Mr Fixit grabbed his tail. The thick black fur was soft and slippery. Mr Fixit lost his grip, staggered back and fell, crash, against the wall. The stars he saw as he banged his head seemed like millions of mocking cats' eyes.

Outside the cats swayed high above the city. Below, the cars and buses and people looked like mechanical toys. The clock in nearby Albert Square struck twelve. The sonorous chimes seemed to reverberate right through their bodies.

'I'm Jim. I'd best get you down then,' said the window cleaner. 'You seem to be in a spot of bother.'

'Purr,' said Madoc.

'Growl,' said Geraint.

'Always do a cat a good turn, that's my motto,' said Jim. 'Anyway, this is a cat's cradle so it's only right I should have cats in it, don't you think?'

'Purr.'

'Growl.'

'What's up with you, Brownie? Haven't you got a civil tongue in your head, growling when I've just saved your life?'

'I don't like this cradle thing,' moaned Geraint with a long yowl. 'I'm a cat, not a cormorant. I feel sick.'

'Hold on, we're nearly down now,' said Jim as he lowered the cradle towards the ground.

'Where are your manners, Geraint? Say "purr" to Jim, that's an order,' snapped Madoc.

'Purr, grrr,' said Geraint.

'Right, jump, the pair of you, and scarper before they catch you.'

'Purrs a million,' said Madoc. 'We won't forget your kindness.'

The two cats ran like the wind. 'Look, there's a

sign to the Greyhound Stadium,' said Madoc. 'Quick, jump on the back of this lorry.'

Luck was with them again. The lorry took them all the way, even stopping at traffic lights just opposite their destination so they didn't have to risk another of their nine lives jumping from a moving vehicle.

On the track the dogs were limbering up for the evening's racing.

'There she is, there's Miss Kip,' miaowed Madoc as a golden streak rushed past him. 'Miss Kip, stop, it's us, Madoc and Geraint!'

Kip wheeled about with such agility and speed that the cats scarcely knew what was happening.

'Madoc, Geraint, darlings! Lovely to see you!' she barked, running up and licking them all over their whiskers. 'I'm a star now, you know. Come and watch me tonight. All my fans and the press photographers and the television cameras will be there. I'm on *Panorama* next week and Hollywood want to make a film and . . .'

'Kip,' said Madoc, 'we've come to take you home.'

'But home's boring and here I'm a star. And this is the most important greyhound track in the country. It was the first ever in Britain, opened in 1926. Only the best dogs race here.'

'I don't doubt that you run well,' said Madoc, 'but be sensible. This life can only end in sadness, Dartington's told you that. Once your racing days are over you'll be on the scrapheap or worse.'

'Worse, I'd say,' growled Geraint.

'I'm a star,' barked Miss Kip, 'I'm not like other hounds, nothing nasty will happen to me.'

'Nobody wants an ex-star. Get out while you can. Come home,' begged Madoc. 'We need you.'

'I'm a star,' barked Miss Kip.

'Esmerelda's had kittens. Wouldn't you like to see them?' said Geraint, knowing Kip's fondness for young creatures.

'I'm a star,' barked Miss Kip.

'And Tessa's not well,' added Madoc, playing his trump card.

'What, the little girl? Tessa? My friend Tessa?' asked Kip.

'Yes, she's not been well since you left and I don't think she'll get better without you. That's what her mam, says, anyway,' said Madoc.

'She won't get better?' asked Kip, her brown eyes wide, her black nose quivering.

'Not without you,' said Madoc.

'Growl,' said Geraint.

'But I'm a st . . .,' began Kip. 'No, who cares about being a star? Jump on my back, let's go!'

The cats had never experienced a journey like it. With their paws wrapped round Kip's chest and stomach they hurtled back towards the railway station, darting round corners, dodging pedestrians and traffic. They heard police sirens. Were they being chased?

On to the platform. The Llanfairpwll train, with Alun at the engine, was waiting.

'This is a station announcement,' a voice boomed from the tannoy. 'A dangerous greyhound has escaped. Passengers are advised not to approach this animal. She may bite. The railway company takes no responsibility for the late departure of all trains consequent upon this incident.'

Alun saw the streak of gold approaching from his driver's cab and, knowing Miss Kip and the cats, guessed what must be happening. He opened the door. 'In here, under there, lie down and keep quiet,' he ordered.

A policeman came up, his notebook open, his pencil ready.

'We're looking for a dangerous dog,' he told Alun. 'Didn't I see something odd and furry looking coming in here?'

'No dangerous dog here,' said Alun truthfully.

Mr Sheckles, the greyhound trainer, came running up the platform, puffing hard. 'Have you caught her?' he said. 'She's my best dog, dangerous, of course, but fast.'

'No dangerous dog here,' said the policeman. 'I'm afraid you've lost her, mate. Give me the details and I'll make a report.'

A crowd of reporters and a television crew arrived on the scene.

'How do you feel, Mr Sheckles?' they asked.

'Sick as a parrot,' he said.

Chapter Nine

The bus dropped Snowy and Scarper off at the Private Entrance to Plas Newydd. Beyond the imposing, castellated gateway was a long drive which they knew would lead them to the Rhododendron Garden. As they passed the Grand Lodge that guarded the entrance a fierce dog began barking.

'Please, Mr Dog, we've come to see Harry the Hawk,' said Snowy politely.

'Right, pass friends,' barked the guard dog whose name was Tomos, 'but paws off the pheasants.'

'Miaow,' said Snowy.

'M-m-mew,' agreed Scarper reluctantly.

It was the end of May, the time of year when the Rhododendron Garden is at its best. Bushes as tall as houses, covered in bell-like clusters of flowers of pink, white and deepest red, rocked gently in the light breeze from the Strait. Above them towered graceful Scots pines.

The cats chose one of the many pathways into the secret garden. Dense foliage of brilliant orange-red made it impossible for them to try any short cuts.

'I've never seen leaves like that before,' mewed Scarper.

'Flame of the Forest, that's what it's called,' Snowy told him. 'You won't see bushes much bigger than those anywhere.'

Some of the rhododendrons were scented and Scarper stopped to sniff. 'Do you mind?' said an angry bee. 'This is my blossom. Buzz off.'

The path took the animals across several small bridges, under which flowed a sparkling stream. 'I wonder if there are any fish in this?' said Snowy. 'I feel a bit peckish.'

'How about catching a pheasant?' said Scarper. 'Just a little one, to keep us going. It seems an awful long time since breakfast.'

A large black bird swooped low over their heads. 'Crraaaa, Craaaa, I'll report you for poaching,' it croaked, 'or I'll tear your eyes out for my own tasty snack.' It was Rhodri Raven, one of several ravens that lived on the estate.

'It's all right, Mr Raven,' said Snowy, 'we were only thinking about food.'

'The thought is father to the deed,' croaked Raymond. 'Don't think I haven't got your measure! Thieving felines!'

He flew off and the cats breathed sighs of relief. A raven was not the sort of bird you wanted to get your claws entangled with.

The path widened to a clearing where the grass was green and soft. 'Just a quick roll,' said little Scarper, running and frisking like a lamb before he rolled over and over. The grass, still wet with dew, cooled his ginger fur. He stretched his legs and white-tipped paws in delight and rubbed his pink nose in the turf.

'Right, Scarper Purr Kitten, enough of this,' said Snowy, taking command. 'This is where we'll find Harry the Hawk. We'd better start caterwauling.'

The two cats stretched their necks, laid back their ears and began their unearthly yowling. 'Harry the Hawk, sir!' they caterwauled in unison. 'We are emissaries from Madoc the Magnificent, Prince of Cats, and we request an audience. Yarrooooh! Yarrooooow!'

They looked upwards, the pupils of their eyes narrowing to slits against the light, but all they could see were wispy white clouds and the tops of the pine trees, some fifty metres above them, their foliage looking like dark lace against the blue sky.

'We'll have to keep trying,' miaowed Snowy Tom. 'He could be anywhere and we can't return to Madoc empty-pawed, so to speak.'

They repeated their performance with renewed vigour.

'Noisy bundles of feline fur,' grumbled an earthworm. 'Thank goodness I haven't got ears.'

Suddenly, as if from nowhere, they saw a great bird hovering high above them somewhere between the clouds and the tree tops. 'Who calls for Harry the Hawk?' cried the bird, and even from a height his voice sounded strong and full of authority.

'It's us, Snowy Tom and Scarper Purr Kitten,' miaowed Snowy at the top of his voice, 'and we've come as ambassadors from Madoc the Magnificent to ask your help.'

Whoosh! It all happened so quickly that the cats couldn't think what was going on. They crouched down in fear, the fur on their backs standing on end, their tails bushed out. In seconds, Harry had dropped from the sky to a spot inches from them. And he didn't seem to have hurt himself at all: even his feathers were unruffled. 'What can I do for you?' he said.

'Well, your Hawkship,' began Snowy, 'it's like this . . .' In a series of miaows and growls he told Harry the whole story of Horatio Hedgehog and his family and friends and how the hognappers planned to take their captives out of the country, to the United States of America, by plane.

'So you're looking for an airfield, a remote airfield,' said Harry. 'Let me think.' He flew to a nearby tree trunk and perched there preening his feathers. It was a great aid to concentration.

'It's a very pleasant spot you've got here,' miaowed Scarper, anxious to please so impressive a bird. 'Have you lived here long?'

'Harry the Hawks have been here for over 200 years,' he replied. 'We've seen it all: the rebuilding of the big house, the time our human, the first Marquess of Anglesey, came home from the war, (against Napoleon that was, at Waterloo, in 1815) without his leg . . .'

'Without his leg? What had he done with it?' mewed Scarper, thinking what bad luck it was on humans, anyway, to have only two legs instead of four like every self-respecting animal.

'He lost it,' said Harry.

'How can you lose your leg? I mean, it's stuck on, isn't it, to the rest of you . . .' mewed Scarper.

'You could have it bitten off by a dog, like Patchwork's tail,' said Snowy.

'Indeed you could,' said Harry, 'but my human's ancestor had his right leg smashed by grape shot on the field of battle. He was in command of the Cavalry. Horses, you know. No tanks in those days. His leg was so bad the surgeon had to cut it off, there and then, and they buried it underneath a willow tree. But he had a wooden one made for him, which moved just as if it had proper joints. It was the first articulated artificial limb and was called The Anglesey Leg. He could even dance with it.'

'Is that the same man as the one on top of the column?' miaowed Snowy.

'That's him, well his statue, anyway. It's a wonderful place to perch on a fine day. See for miles. Which brings me back to your problem, an airfield. Let me think.'

Harry fell silent and preened his feathers, then he spread his wings and leaned back as if relaxing in a comfortable deck chair, his head to one side, his hooded eyes closed – or nearly closed: he wasn't called Hawk-eye for nothing.

'He's a famous military historian,' Snowy told Scarper in muted miaow. 'There's nothing he doesn't know about battles and things. We'd better sit quiet while he concentrates.'

The cats crouched on their haunches, marvelling at how Harry leaned back against nothing but thin air. The bees hummed in the yellow azaleas; a pink rhododendron blossom, as large as a football, dropped from its branch; a rabbit scuttled past, white tail bobbing, and the Scots pines, hundreds of years old, sighed in the breeze and sang, 'Oh, what a beautiful morning!'

At last Harry opened his eyes, folded his wings and perched up straight. Thrusting his beak forward in typical hawk attitude, he said: 'I've got it.'

'Got what, your Hawkship?' miaowed the cats.

'The place those hognappers will use. It's just south of Caernarfon, near a village called Llanwnda. It's quite remote and it's not used a lot but there are a few buildings there and all the facilities, as humans say. Come on, I'll show you.'

'Show us? How?' miaowed the cats.

'I'll fly you there,' said Harry, and then seemed to reconsider his offer. 'Well, I'll fly one of you there. I'll take Scarper.'

'Mew,' said Scarper in great excitement.

Snowy had no wish whatever to fly through the air like a trapeze cat, hanging in undignified suspension from Harry's strong claws, but, as senior cat, he thought he should have been given the option.

'Scarper's only a kitten, your Hawkship, and I am an experienced cat of the world. Shouldn't you take me?'

There were two reasons why Harry didn't want to carry Snowy. One was that he was extremely plump and no doubt very heavy and the other was that he smelt. Harry, somewhat fastidious, didn't fancy having to plunge his clean and finely-honed claws into that grimy, off-white fur.

'It is precisely because you are such an experienced and wise animal that I won't take you,' said Harry, who had once served in the Diplomatic Corps. 'Were I to drop you, it would be an incalcuable loss to the feline world.'

'Of course,' said Snowy.

Scarper thought it would be a pretty incalcuable sort of a loss, to him at any rate, if he were dropped but he was a brave kitten and reckoned that, since he had so far lost only a couple of his nine lives, he could risk a third in the cause of Madoc and a good adventure.

'I'm ready, your Hawkship,' he mewed.

'I'll do a bit of a recce round here and see you back at Dilys's along the road,' said Snowy. 'We can catch the bus for Beaumaris from there.' By now he was decidedly hungry and he knew that, if he stepped on it, Dilys would be serving elevenses: *bara brith*, Welsh cakes and a saucer of full cream milk. It was not to be missed. 'Youth before beauty,' he said to Scarper, waving a grubby paw. 'It's a heavy responsibility being a cat of substance.'

Harry took Scarper in his claws and in no time they were soaring above the pine trees, over the Strait and southwards towards Caernarfon and the open sea. 'Everything looks quite different,' mewed Scarper. 'Is this what they call a bird's eye view?'

'There's the airstrip,' said Harry, 'and there's the reception room they'll probably use. You can get to it by road quite easily. Look, there's the turning. Or you can cut across the fields if you prefer.'

'Mew,' said Scarper, but he had his doubts about finding it again from ground level. .

'Got it?' said Harry. 'Right! About fly!' And he wheeled round on extended wing and flew back across the Strait to Anglesey.

When they arrived at Dilys's, Snowy was only on his second saucer and third Welsh cake. He hadn't even started on the *bara brith*.

'Thank you, your Hawkship,' said Scarper, 'but I'm still not sure I could locate the place without your help.'

'Don't worry, I'll be looking out for you,' said Harry. '*Dim diolch*, Dilys, no thank you, I won't stop for a *paned* now, I've some busy hunting ahead. Must fly.'

With a whoosh of his powerful wings he was off, a handsome and noble bird, lord of the skies.

'Another saucer, did you say, Dilys?' asked Snowy. 'I don't mind if I do.'

Chapter 10

Tessa's bedroom door was ajar. Kip pushed it open with her nose and padded softly in. Tessa lay in bed, her fair hair scraped back from her brow, which, Kip could see, had beads of sweat on it. Her eyes were closed, her cheeks were flushed and she was breathing heavily.

Kip walked over to the bed and put her nose gently on the blankets. She made no noise as she didn't wish to wake Tessa. She knew from her mother that she had had a bad night and had only just got off to sleep. The doctor would call later that morning.

After a few minutes Tessa stirred, coughed a little and her eyes fluttered open. 'Miss Kip,' she said, 'is it you? Is it really you?' She put out her hand to touch Kip's head to make sure she wasn't dreaming. Kip nuzzled up and licked her. How hot her hand was and how quickly the pulse beat in her wrist.

'Yes, it's me,' she said in a very soft bark. 'I came home when I heard how ill you were. It was wrong of me to stay away so long. I'm sorry, Tessa. Please get well.'

'I will now, Kip, I will. And we'll play on the beach and go for walks in the woods and you can sit with me while I do my homework.'

'Bark,' said Kip, and putting her front paws on the bed, she licked Tessa all over her face.

95

'Kip, what are you doing?' cried Tessa's mother, coming into the room. 'Be careful, you'll give her germs.'

'No, Mam, I feel much better,' said Tessa, and, oddly enough, she looked it.

'Bark, bark,' said Kip, meaning she would have to go out for a few hours to help Madoc on an Important Mission.

'But you'll come back?' asked Tessa, tears welling up in her eyes. 'Promise you'll come back.'

'I promise,' barked Kip, and she vowed that the days of wine and roses were behind her forever. What was fame compared to a loving family? How could the adulation of the crowd, the glare of the television lights, the constant clicking of the paparazzi's cameras ever make up for a secure home and affection freely given?

The sound of footsteps on the stairs was followed by a light knock on the door.

'Good morning, doctor,' said Tessa's mother.

'And how's the patient today?' asked the doctor, taking out his stethoscope.

'A bit better,' said Tessa, which, in itself, was an improvement since she hadn't been able to talk at all the day before.

'She had a bad night, then at last this morning she got off to sleep, I left her for a few minutes and Miss Kip arrived and when I got back she seemed brighter,' said Tessa's mother in a rush.

The doctor listened to the girl's chest, took her temperature and felt her pulse. 'A great improvement, little lady,' he said. 'You're over the worst now.' Turning to her mother, he added, 'Another couple of days in bed, some light meals, plenty to drink, carry on with the tablets and she'll be as right as rain. It's odd, you said she was pining for her dog, and now Miss Kip has come home, Tessa has definitely taken a turn for the better. Even with the great advances in medical science today we don't have all the answers. Now, don't go running off again, Miss Kip,' he said, turning to the golden greyhound.

'Bark,' said Miss Kip.

'Good dog,' said Tessa, and smiled as she hadn't smiled for over a week.

Chapter 11

An emergency Council of Cats was called for the 30th of May. Miss Kip was there as an Honorary Cat and Horatio Hedgehog attended in his capacity as 'interested party'. Patchwork, who had been in charge in Beaumaris while Madoc was away, undertook to record the minutes. He did them in his head because he was not a literate cat like Great Uncle Marmaduke and could neither read nor write.

'Thanks to a magnificent team effort, we now know the villains' plan,' Madoc told the Council. 'We know which airport they are using, we know the time of the meeting and we know they will be stopping for half an hour or so for bacon butties in the reception room. All that remains is to work out our own rescue plan and to achieve the release of the victims without any casualties among cat, hound or hog.'

Horatio Hedgehog started to gruntle. 'If there are going to be casualties, body bags and so on, I wish I'd never asked for help.'

'And I wish we'd never given it,' grumbled Geraint. 'You've done nothing but moan and eat, and eat and moan, since you arrived. That old-fashioned word "gruntling" for "grumbling" just suits you. You're a right disgruntled misery.'

'And you're a skinny, scrawny, bad-tempered old mog,' retorted Horatio, his voice becoming loud and hysterical.

'Order!' called Madoc. 'We have no time to lose in bandying insults. This is my plan.'

Horatio and Geraint were still gruntling and growling. 'Silence for Madoc the Magnificent!' ordered Patchwork, and lashed what was left of his tail.

'First of all, Horatio, I want you to round up all the hedgehogs in the area and get them to donate a prickle each,' said Madoc.

'But we can't have gaps in our prickles,' protested Horatio. 'They're our protection against predators.'

'Don't be ridiculous, Horatio,' said Madoc sternly. 'You know as well as I do that the average hedgehog has 5,000 spines. What is one among five thousand? And, anyway, they are like hair and fur: they'll grow again.'

'I suppose so,' gruntled Horace, 'but it'll be painful getting them out. I don't know if I can see my way . . .'

'It's a poor show if you can't go through a little pain and suffering to save your fellow hogs from an unpleasant and lingering death,' interrupted Madoc. 'We know that hogs who are taken to the United States cannot adapt to the climate. That's why it's a hogless land; for some reason they simply can't live there. And if you and your fellow hogs who live in liberty and luxury in this happy land refuse to give one single prickle from the thousands on your back, then these hapless hogs – many of them, may I remind you, of your own flesh and blood – are doomed to an untimely and miserable end. Shame on you, Horatio, for being such a heartless hog.'

'Well, if you put it that way, Madoc, sir, I'll see what I can do,' squeaked Horatio. 'But what are you going to do with our prickles, may I ask, and who is going to pull them out?'

'In answer to your second question, we cats will pull them out with our teeth . . .'

'Eeeeeeek,' squeaked Horatio.

'And the reason we want them is to make some nice, spiky cushions.'

'I don't see why we should be part of an upholstery project.' Horatio was gruntling again, but seeing Madoc's flashing amber eyes and the curl of his lip as he snarled, he quickly changed gruntle to squeak. 'Oh, all right, if you say so,' he said.

'The spiky cushions are part of my Grand Rescue Plan,' continued Madoc. 'It should work well and disable all the villains including the pilot. But we need some strong animals to keep our quarry in the reception room while we go about our work. We'll need a good hour, I would say. Any ideas, Miss Kip, who might help?'

'Some animal stronger than me, you mean?' barked Kip.

'Yes, no offence,' said Madoc, 'but you're not exactly bulky. We need at least a couple of animals with big paws and sharp teeth and lots of weight behind them. Remember, they need to be able to restrain at least four grown men.'

'Let me think,' said Kip, and covered her face with her paws. After a few seconds she raised her head, her intelligent brown eyes shining. 'I have just the animals,' she said. 'Two puppies . . .'

'Puppies!' exclaimed Geraint. 'How stupid can you be! Only a dog could be silly enough to suggest puppies when asked to provide something big and strong. I know two kittens who'd hold up a bank if you asked them . . .'

'Don't be rude about kittens,' mewed Scarper. 'We can't help being young, and one day we'll grow up and you'll be old, and then you'll be sorry.'

'Silence!' growled Madoc. 'Let Miss Kip speak.'

'These puppies to whom I refer,' said Kip with dignity, 'are not cute little bundles of fur. They are as big as human men and just as strong. They are loving and amiable, like all the best hounds, and they won't hurt you cats, but they've got enormous jaws, and teeth even longer than mine, and their growl is so low and menacing it would freeze your blood. I'll be happy to approach them on your behalf, Madoc, if you so wish.'

'They sound as if they may be our dogs,' replied Madoc, 'but how old are they exactly? Are they disciplined, are they reliable? What sort of dogs are they?'

'Bloodhounds,' barked Kip. 'Nine months old, as tall as a man and weighing about 40 kilograms a piece. Paws like lions, jaws like crocodiles. And so eager to please that they'll do anything you ask.'

'What are their names?' said Madoc.

'Amy and Minnie. Amy is red and Minnie is black and tan and . . .'

'Amy and Minnie!' chortled Geraint (a cat can chortle, just about). 'They sound a right wimpish pair. And bitches too! Useless!'

'Do you mind?' growled Miss Kip. 'Bitches are every bit as good as dogs and, what's more, they are not so easily distracted. Dogs! Only one thing on their mind, if you ask me.'

'What's that?' mewed Scarper.

'Lady dogs, of course,' explained Patchwork. 'Now stop interrupting. Kittens should be seen and not heard.'

'Thank you, Patchwork,' said Madoc. He turned to Kip. 'How soon could these hounds be ready?'

'Within minutes. They only live up the road, the only bloodhounds in this part of Wales. And may I just add,' she growled, turning scathing brown eyes on Geraint, 'that these hounds have proper pedigree names as well, Weatheroak Earlybird and Weatheroak Elysia, but we couldn't expect an uneducated cat like you to be able to pronounce names like that, let alone remember them.'

The hair rose on Geraint's scrawny back. He advanced towards Kip, teeth bared in a hideous grimace.

'Geraint! Kip! Stop it this minute!' ordered Madoc. 'How are we to get anywhere if we keep quarrelling among ourselves? Kip, bring Amy and Minnie here. Horatio, round up your hogs. Cats, sharpen your teeth in preparation for prickle-pulling. I declare this meeting closed.'

Chapter Twelve

Alf and Gwilym were making bacon butties in the bedsit in Caernarfon they had rented as a base for their operations. In another much smaller room off the bedsit five hundred unhappy hedgehogs cowered in makeshift cages, cramped, cold and hungry.

Hedgehogs have an acute sense of smell and the aroma of frying bacon that wafted towards their prison cell was too much to bear. Soon they were all squealing, a frightening, piercing, piglike squeal.

'Shut them up, Gwil, or we'll have our neighbours complaining,' said Alf. 'We can't afford to have anything go wrong at this late stage in the game.'

'I'll turn up the tele, that'll drown the noise,' said Gwilym. 'Or should we give them some of our bacon? They must be hungry.'

'And you must be off your rocker. What, waste food on a pile of prickles when we'll be rid of them in less than twelve hours? Do me a favour.'

A knock came on the door. It was Mrs Jones from the room above wanting to know what was going on. 'Are you all right?' she asked in Welsh. '*Ydy popeth yn iawn?*'

Gwilym answered her in the same language, which, being his first language, he spoke with greater ease than English. He assured her that it was only some horror film on the video and refused her kind offer of a '*paned o de*', a cup of tea.

'What was all that about?' asked Alf crossly. 'I suppose you were talking about me. It's always the same when you lot get together. Why do you want to speak that crazy language anyway? Why can't you speak sensible English like the rest of us?'

Gwilym was angry. Insulting his language was as bad as insulting his mother. 'I wasn't speaking about you. What on earth would I want to do that for? It's my language and I have every right to speak it. It's not crazy either. People who know about these things, which is more than you do, say it's more logical than English and it's easier to spell too. So there! And if you don't like not being able to understand, why don't you learn? I learnt English.'

The argument had diverted Alf's attention from his bacon and the fat in the pan was smoking badly. 'Look out, you'll set the place on fire if you're not careful,' warned Gwilym.

'At least it's stopped those hogs squealing their prickles off,' grumbled Alf. 'Now let's get a move on. Shove that burnt slice between two bits of bread and no one will know the difference. That's what I was told as a kid. If it's disgusting and you've got to eat it, put it between bread.'

Two large sliced loaves were converted into bacon sandwiches, liberally laced with brown sauce. 'Now for the coffee,' said Alf. 'You got them thermoses?'

'Here,' said Gwilym.

'Right, you spoon in the granules while I pour on the hot water. We'll take the milk and sugar separately.'

'I hope nothing goes wrong,' said Gwilym.

'It can't,' said Alf. 'Anyway, there's no law says you can't collect hedgehogs, kindly like.'

'No, I suppose not,' said Gwilym.

'And there's nothing in law neither to say as how you can't send them to America, now is there?'

'No, I suppose not,' repeated Gwilym miserably. He knew vaguely that some law had been passed to protect wild life, including hogs, against cruelty but whether that meant you couldn't fly them to America was beyond him. All he knew was that it didn't feel right.

He had another reason for feeling miserable. He had read his weekly horoscope in the paper that morning and it warned him that the full moon that night would bring matters to a head. 'Your plans may be upset by an unknown agent,' it read. 'You may find yourself in an embarrassing situation, you could even end up in hospital. Don't make any social or romantic plans for the weekend.'

'Couldn't we just call the whole thing off?' he asked.

'What and lose our money from Mr Fixit and the chance of more jobs? What's got into you? No, we can't call it off.'

'No, I suppose not,' said Gwilym.

'Right, let's get a bit of shut eye before we have to pack up these miserable squealers and be on our way. Cheer up, in a few hours' time we'll be rich. A much surer thing than the lottery and we might win that too.'

'I suppose so,' said Gwilym, but he was full of foreboding. He went to the window and drew back the curtain. In a deep navy sky the full moon shone yellow and bright. A clock in the town chimed midnight and an owl hooted. In the yard below Gwilym saw something move. It was a mouse. Even though he was two floors up he could see the shape of the creature clearly in the moonlight. There was a whoosh of wings, a flurry of white feathers and the mouse was gone. The owl flew off silently to devour his prey. Was it an omen, thought Gwilym?

Chapter Thirteen

'Why can't we just go the police and let them deal with the matter?' grumbled Geraint Growler. 'My mouth's sore from pulling out prickles and there's a good rat-hunt on tonight in Menai Bridge, down by the pier. Great sport, my mates tell me. Why should I miss that to help a load of spikey snivellers?'

'Because, Geraint, you are a Steel Town Cat and your word is your bond,' said Madoc, amber eyes flashing. 'And because,' he added, 'I say so.'

Patchwork ran up, his multi-coloured coat tousled and covered in burrs from a recent stalking expedition. 'Sam says, be ready to leave in ten minutes,' he miaowed.

Sam, Miss Kip's human and Tessa's father, had agreed to give the animals a lift as far as just beyond Caernarfon. They didn't want him to take them to the 'scene of the crime' as they weren't absolutely sure he would approve of their activities. And Sam knew better than to ask them what they were about. All he would get would be sidelong glances and a mysterious 'brrrrrp, brrrrrp'. As usual in his relations with the Steel Town Cats, he just had to trust them.

'Let me explain again why we can't go to the police,' said Madoc. 'And listen this time, Geraint! No catnapping! Although hedgehogs have some protection in law, we don't know quite how much.

108

We don't know if the police would have powers of arrest and whether the villains would be punished in an appropriate fashion. That's why we animals have to take it into our own paws to rescue the hogs, stop this cruel trade and see that the villains get their just desserts.'

'How do we do that?' mewed Scarper.

'Wait and see. It's all part of my Prickly Plan,' said Madoc.

'A Prickly Plan for a Prickly Problem,' miaowed Patchwork.

'Quite,' growled his chief. 'Now where are Miss Kip and the hounds? Sam won't want to hang around.'

Scarcely had he finished speaking than a thunder of paws was heard and two enormous puppies, with drooping jowls, long floppy ears and more wrinkles than you'd see on a prune, bounded into the garden. Their strong tails, more correctly called sterns, wagged so fiercely that within seconds they had knocked over several plant pots and an assortment of garden furniture. Fortunately the cats themselves were well below tail level or they, too, would have been sent flying by the hyper-enthusiastic waggers. Miss Kip, slender and elegant, trotted behind. 'Let me introduce Amy and Minnie,' she said. 'I've explained their role to them and they are more than eager to help, as you can see.'

'We want to help as much as we can and all we want in return is love,' said Amy.

'Just tell us we're good hounds and we'll be so happy we'll die for you,' sang Minnie. (Bloodhounds do sing: it's a high-pitched sort of hum.)

'You're certainly big enough,' said Madoc. 'I hope you'll fit in Sam's van.'

Sam came out carrying a suitcase. He was going to Cardiff for a few days on business and had delayed leaving home, which he loved, for as long as he could. It was getting dark and the full moon was already high in the sky. The man in it seemed to wink at Madoc and give him the thumbs up sign.

'Surely you don't want me to take those great big bloodhounds as well?' said Sam.

'Purr,' said Madoc.

'Bark,' said Miss Kip.

'And those funny packages?' queried Sam, indicating two large black plastic bags, out of which spikey things protruded. They were, of course, Madoc's collection of prickles.

'Purr,' said Madoc.

'Bark,' said Miss Kip.

'Oh, all right, in you get. What, and Horatio Hedgehog too? Thank goodness Esmerelda is staying home with her kittens or the place would be deserted.'

'Perhaps I should stay and look after her?' suggested Snowy Tom. He didn't much fancy this particular adventure as it seemed they would be unlikely to be near a source of food. Also he knew that Tessa was giving Esmerelda extra snacks to build up her strength after the pregnancy. Surely an animal who had just become a father needed a little nurturing too? In a world of equal opportunities, was not a nursing father as entitled to special care as a nursing mother? 'I feel duty calls,' he miaowed.

'Duty, my back paw,' growled Geraint. 'Sloth and greed, more like. I know your game . . .'

'Silence!' said Madoc. 'Snowy, you come with us. We need every cat we can muster.'

111

The bloodhounds got into the van first, the packages in their mouths. Miss Kip followed and then the cats piled in, draping themselves over all three hounds.

'Oooh, that's lovely and warm,' said Amy, the bigger of the two puppies. 'What cosy fur you cats have. Yes, Scarper, scratch my head, lick my ears! That's woo-woo-woo-wonderful,' she bayed.

A few miles south of Caernarfon Madoc tapped Sam on the shoulder with his paw. 'This will do, thank you Sam,' he miaowed.

Sam drew into a lay-by and let the animals out. 'Whatever you're up to, be careful,' he said. 'And mind the traffic, it's particularly dangerous at night.'

'Purr,' said Madoc.

'Bark,' said Kip.

'Squeak,' added Horatio Hedgehog.

Once Sam had left them the animals turned off the main road and started to cut across country towards the coast.

'This is the way Harry the Hawk showed me,' said Scarper. 'He said it wouldn't take long even on paw.'

'Some animal had better give Horatio a lift,' said Madoc. 'He can't run as fast as we can even though he's much swifter on his feet than I imagined.'

'Let me,' said Amy, sitting down so Horatio could climb on. 'Hold onto my ears and you'll be just fine. But no rolling over, I don't want to be scratched by your spines.'

'I'll try and be careful,' said Horatio, 'but if a prickle does get out of place you can always bark.'

'And if she barks she'll drop the bag of prickles she's carrying,' said Madoc, tail lashing. 'They could fall down a cliff or into a river and then where would we be? Horatio, you must not scratch Amy, is that understood?'

'Squeak.'

Minnie, who was carrying the second bag of prickles in her mouth, put it down and asked, 'May I give any animal a lift? I love being helpful, that's what I love best of all in the whole world.'

'Yes,' said Madoc, 'Scarper's only a kitten, he could do with a lift.'

'I'm all right, Madoc,' protested Scarper. 'I'm a big kitten now and I'm as strong as any cat. I can keep up.'

'I'll take your kind offer, Minnie, if Scarper doesn't want it,' miaowed Snowy Tom. 'I've always fancied travelling in a howdah.'

'Don't be ridiculous, Snowy,' growled Madoc. 'Howdahs are seats on the backs of elephants, not bloodhounds. And we're in Wales, not India. You'll use the paws the Great Cat gave you like the rest of us. Scarper,' he added, turning to the rebellious ginger kitten, 'I don't want you getting tired. Climb on Minnie's back this instant before I show you the rough side of my claw.'

By the light of the silvery moon the procession of animals made its way through woodland, over fields and across streams. All sorts of animals were about that night: foxes, shrews, bats, owls.

Suddenly Horatio let out a bloodcurdling scream. Amy dropped her bag of prickles and bayed in terror. Minnie did the same, while Scarper, not wishing to disobey Madoc, clung to her fur trying not to dig his claws in too deep. Miss Kip and the adult cats froze, hackles up, ears pricked, whiskers extended, eyes alert.

'What is it?' growled Madoc softly.

'Badgers,' squeaked Horatio hysterically, 'I smell badgers. They'll pull me apart with their long claws and eat me. Oh, that I had been hognapped with my companions and sent to America. Better to try and survive in a hogless land than be eaten alive. Oh, hapless, helpless, hopeless hog!'

'Hopeless is just about it,' growled Madoc. 'You could wreck our plan with your silly squealing. Of course there are badgers around, it's night-time and they're nocturnal animals, but even the stupidest badger is hardly likely to take on a greyhound, two bloodhounds and the Steel Town Cats for the sake of one measly hedgehog.'

'Measly? Measle? Me?' spluttered Horatio.

'Weasel, did you say? Weasels can't get measles and measles can't get weasels. But cats can. The cat's got the measles, the measles, the chicken-pox, The cat's got the measles, the measles got the the cat!'

A high-pitched voice, coming from somewhere on the woodland floor, sang out the old nursery rhyme. Then it added, 'Pop. Pop goes the what?'

'The weasel, of course! Wilbert Weasel, my old

friend,' squeaked Horatio. 'Good to see you again, except that I can't. See you, that is.'

'They seek him here, they seek him there, those hoglets seek him everywhere . . .' sang Wilbert.

'Wilbert, I'm Miss Kip, the golden greyhound. We've met before, I believe, on your farm just a few miles from here. These are my friends, Madoc the Magnificent and his Steel Town Cats, and Amy and Minnie, the bloodhound puppies. We're looking for an airport. Can you help us?'

'I'm walking in the air.' Wilbert started to sing again.

'You have a charming voice,' said Madoc, skilled in diplomacy from his days in Number 10 Downing Street. 'If you can help us we'd be most grateful. We're on a very important mission.'

'Then I'm your weasel,' said Wilbert. 'Pop!' And he popped up in front of the bemused animals, standing on his hind legs, his lithe red body swaying as he spoke, his head erect, his front paws extended. If the Royal Ballet auditioned animals Wilbert would have got the job. 'This way!' he squeaked.

Scarper looked up and in the light of the breaking dawn he saw, far above, the outline of a great bird. It was Harry the Hawk making sure, as he had promised, that he would see they were all right.

Chapter Fourteen

Wilbert Weasel knew exactly where the airfield was. It was not big enough to be called an airport like Cardiff, Manchester or Heathrow. There were perhaps half a dozen hangars and a runway, an air traffic control tower and a reception building that looked rather like a cricket pavilion.

'That's where they'll meet up and have their sandwiches,' said Wilbert, and then, once again, he burst into song. 'Hot cross buns, hot cross buns, one a penny, two a penny, hot cross buns . . .'

'Buns?' mewed Scarper. 'I thought you said sandwiches.'

'Well, I did,' said Wilbert, annoyed, 'but I can't think of any rhyme or song that has sandwiches in it, can you?'

'N-not really,' said Scarper, wracking his brains to find something to rhyme with sandwiches.

'Animals! Your attention, please!' ordered Madoc the Magnificent. 'We're here to do an important job, not make up verses. Amy, Minnie, have you got your bags of prickles?'

'Bark,' said Amy and Minnie in unison.

'I haven't revealed the details of the Rescue Plan to you before because the utmost secrecy has been required,' said Madoc. 'Now Patchwork will tell you exactly what each of you must do. Listen carefully. Patchwork!'

The multi-coloured cat stepped forward. 'Our timing must be exact,' he said. 'The aircraft is due to land at six hundred hours, by which time Alf and Gwilym will have arrived with their shameful cargo of hedgehogs. Their boss, Mr Fixit, from the headquarters of Just Ask in Manchester, has arranged to meet them here for coffee and bacon butties . . .'

'What are butties?' squeaked Wilbert.

'Sandwiches,' said Snowy Tom. 'Every animal knows that. But, alas, I don't like bread; I only like the filling. And I wish humans wouldn't mess up their food with vinegar and mayonnaise and mustard and sauce and things. Can give a cat quite a nasty turn, can mustard . . .'

'Snowy, stop thinking of your stomach, just for once,' ordered Madoc, tail lashing. 'We'll get a good feast when we get home. Tessa has promised us that. Please continue, Patchwork!'

'They will meet in the Reception Room, as Wilbert said . . .'

'Squeak,' said Wilbert.

'. . . and when the pilot lands he will join them for a break, having first checked that his cargo, in other words the consignment of hogs, is all present and correct. Alf and Gwilym will load the crates on board and then, for thirty minutes, no more, all four villains plan to be in that building, eating their butties. They will then board the plane for the Republic of Ireland.'

'Ireland? Eire?' squeaked Horatio. 'I thought you said they were destined for America. Ireland's a nice place for hogs, lots of rain, lots of slugs, and fat worms, too.'

'So we've been on a wild goose, or wild hog, chase then,' grumbled Geraint Growler. 'All this painful work pulling prickles and the stupid hogs are only going as far as Ireland.'

'There's good racing in Ireland,' barked Miss Kip, who had been silent on this journey, her head full of memories of her recent days of fame and glory. 'Perhaps I should go with them and investigate?'

'Shame on you, Miss Kip, for a faithless hound!' Madoc rebuked her. 'Remember your promise to Tessa.' Miss Kip hung her head and rolled her eyes. 'Please continue, Patchwork.'

'Mr Fixit, Alf and Gwilym only plan to fly as far as Ireland,' miaowed Patchwork. 'The hogs, after transference to a larger aircraft, will continue their journey . . .'

'So you're letting them take my relations and friends to America after all?' squeaked Horatio. 'I knew it was no good asking cats for help. I don't know why Uncle Hywel suggested it. He always was a silly old buffer.'

'And I've missed an ace rat-hunt in Menai Bridge for nothing,' grumbled Geraint.

'I haven't finished yet,' said Patchwork tersely. 'If you'll stop squeaking and growling and gruntling and give me a chance, I'll explain.' The animals fell silent. 'While the villains are having their butties, we cats get to work with the prickles. I'll explain exactly what to do later. But it may take us longer than thirty minutes and this is where you, Amy, and you, Minnie, come in.'

'Whaaaaa,' bayed Amy and Minnie in unison.

'By the pricking of my thumbs, something wicked this way comes,' said Horatio, who had once heard a human reciting the famous lines from *Macbeth* and liked to use them when the occasion demanded. In common with the rest of his species, Horatio's hearing was exceptionally acute. He could even hear a worm coming out of the ground. So the distant hum of an approaching engine was easily picked up. Soon the other animals heard it too.

'They're coming,' said Madoc. 'Take cover! We'll hear the rest of the instructions in hiding.'

Alf and Gwilym were the first to arrive in their shabby Lada van. They drew up next to the Reception Room, unloaded their breakfast picnic of coffee and sandwiches and went inside to shelter from the chill of the morning air, leaving the crated hogs behind in the vehicle.

'Why don't we go and rescue them now and get it over so's I can get back for the end of the rat-hunt?' said Geraint Growler.

'Quiet,' ordered Madoc. 'We must keep to our plan, it's the only way.'

The sound of another, much quieter engine was heard and soon Mr Fixit's Volvo joined Alf's van on the tarmac. 'Morning, boys,' he said as his two henchmen came out to greet him. 'Got the butties? I'm starving.'

119

Before the three men had time to enter the building a droning sound signalled the imminent arrival of the light aircraft that was to carry them across the Celtic Sea to Ireland. The plane bumped down on the runway and braked to a halt, not all that far from the cats' hiding place. The pilot undid his safety belt, lowered the steps and climbed out.

'Right, let's get the merchandise on board and then we can relax,' said the pilot, whose name was Bill. 'I'll just check that it's alive and kicking. Can't pay for dead material, can we?'

'No dead material here, I assure you,' said Mr Fixit. 'Nothing but the best from Just Ask, that's our motto.'

Bill went over to the van and had a quick look through the crates. 'Everthing seems to be in order,' he said. 'Now how's about those bacon butties you promised?'

As Patchwork had predicted, Alf and Gwilym loaded the crates onto the plane and then joined the others in the reception hut.

'Action stations!' ordered Madoc.

The animals knew exactly what to do. Amy and Minnie carried their bags of prickles over to the aircraft before taking up offensive positions outside the hut. Miss Kip helped the cats, Madoc the Magnificent, Patchwork, Snowy, Geraint Growler and Scarper Purr Kitten, into the cockpit. Horatio and Wilbert stood by and prepared to act as a Reception Committee.

'But how can we get the hogs out of their crates in time before the villains come back?' mewed Scarper. 'It'll take ages to open them, even with the sharpest of claws.' He was a practical animal for all his few short months.

'I've thought of that,' said Madoc. 'We don't need to open the crates at all. All we have to do is get these prickles inserted in the seating and then those rogues will be glad to do anything we ask them, you'll see.'

The cats worked with speed placing the spikes in the seat cushions. They did it so cleverly that even an eagle-eyed bird like Harry the Hawk would not have noticed their presence.

But it took time. Thirty minutes was up. The men in the hut prepared to leave.

It was the bloodhounds' signal for action. Amy and Minnie jumped up at the glass door, baring their teeth and growling. Although only nine months old, they were as big as the men and more powerful. The rims of their eyes were red and their fleshy jowls dripped slobber, as though slavering in anticipation of a feast of human flesh.

'It must be those butties that's attracted them,' said Mr Fixit. 'What did you put in them, you fool?'

'Only HP sauce,' said Alf. 'It's never had that effect before, I promise you.'

'I must get back to my plane,' said Bill. 'If we leave those hogs hanging around too long they'll die and I'll be badly out of pocket.'

'And if we try to get out of here we'll die,' said Mr

Fixit. 'Look at those teeth and those whacking great paws and claws. Hell hounds! Isn't that just my luck?'

Amy and Minnie kept up their snarling until a signal from Miss Kip told them that the cats had finished their work. They withdrew their front paws from the door, stood back and starting singing in the strange way bloodhounds do.

'I think they're all right now,' said Gwilym. 'They are going to let us through.'

'How can you be sure?' asked Mr Fixit.

'I know about hounds,' replied Gwilym, 'brought up with them. They are all right for the moment, anyway.'

'Well, let's strike while the iron's hot, I say,' said Bill. 'Come on!'

They opened the door and, escorted on either side by Amy and Minnie, the four men walked to the aircraft.

'Whaaaa,' bayed Amy and Minnie, indicating they should board. 'Bark,' said Miss Kip, reinforcing the order.

'There's another wretched dog,' grumbled Mr Fixit. 'What is this place, an animal sanctuary?'

The four men climbed inside, sat down and . . .

Their screams, as the hedgehogs' prickles buried themselves deep in the soft flesh of their backsides, could be heard in the village five miles away.

'Ouwwwww,' cried Mr Fixit.

'Ooooooooo,' bellowed Bill.

'Ouch, ouch, ouch,' exploded Alf as the sharp spines dug deep.

'Duw, o Duw, the pain,' moaned Gwilym.

The four had risen from their seats, indeed they had jumped up pretty smartly, but the spiky cushions remained firmly embedded in their posteriors.

'Well, don't just stand there whimpering, Alf, Gwilym. Do something!' said Mr Fixit. 'Get hold of the corners of this blasted cushion and pull.'

Alf and Gwilym started to pull but the spines had twisted in the flesh and they wouldn't budge. Mr Fixit cried out in agony. 'Be careful, you oafs, you'll have my guts out. Ouuuuwwwww!'

'Guts for garters,' squeaked Wilbert, who, with the cats, Horatio, Miss Kip, Amy and Minnie, was observing the scene from below.

'Ooooooo, I think I'm going to faint,' said Bill. 'Let's get out of here and summon medical assistance. We don't know what these things are. They could be spiked with venom and we'll all die.'

'Go to the telephone, Alf, and dial 999. It's our only chance,' said Mr Fixit. 'Right, everyone out!'

'No, you don't,' miaowed the authoritative voice of Madoc the Magnificent. 'Get back inside and do as I say or I'll set the hounds on you.'

Amy and Minnie growled menacingly and bared their teeth. But one aspect of their performance displeased Miss Kip and she gave an angry bark. 'Stop wagging your tails, you silly puppies. If the humans see that they won't believe you're as fierce as you look.'

123

'Well, we're not,' said Amy. 'Our bark is a lot worse than our bite, you know that, and we'd much rather be friends.'

'Yes, can we be friends now,' interrupted Minnie, 'now that it's all over?'

'It's not all over,' barked Kip angrily. 'Get growling, raise your hackles and keep those tails under control. Your job is only half done.'

Fortunately, the men had been so transfixed by the sight of the hounds' fiercesome sets of teeth that they hadn't noticed the wagging tails.

'I don't believe it,' groaned Mr Fixit, focusing on Madoc and Geraint Growler. 'It's those mouldy mogs that came to the office in Manchester and made me crash my head on the wall. I've not been right since. I knew they was trouble as soon as I clapped eyes on them.'

'And there's that dirty white thing that made a filthy smell on our nice clean trousers,' said Alf.

'And the little ginger one I stopped you throwing in the River Conwy,' added Gwilym. 'There's gratitude!'

Mr Fixit was getting desperate. 'What do you want?' he demanded of Madoc. 'Can't you see we're in agony? We need a doctor. And quickly.'

'You didn't care about inflicting pain on those poor innocent hedgehogs you've got crated up in the back,' said Madoc. 'Now you can suffer a bit.'

'But what if we've been poisoned?' moaned Bill, who was not over-brave. 'We'll all die in agony.'

'Tough,' said Madoc. 'That would have been the fate of these hogs once they got to America, and well you know it. You were quite prepared to send them to certain death just to make a few dollars. Why should we worry about you?'

'Because we're human beings,' said Mr Fixit. 'Our lives are important.'

'And the lives of animals are not?' queried Madoc.

'Not compared to ours, of course not,' retorted Mr Fixit crossly. Madoc spoke human language so well that the unfortunate Fixit, confused by the pain in his rear end, had quite forgotten he was conversing with a cat. 'No, animals exist only for our convenience. They're inferior, you see, no intellect, no souls.'

'I see,' said Madoc, tail lashing. 'And do you, Mr Fixit, include us cats in that generalisation?'

'Ye . . .,' began Mr Fixit, and then realised with horror what he had been saying. 'Oh, sorry, your Grace, your Worship, your Furriness, your . . .'

'Stop gassing, for goodness sake, and ask him what he wants before we all kick the bucket,' said Bill. 'I'm sure my wounds are going septic already.'

'Well, your Honour, what can we do for you?' said Mr Fixit.

'Undo the crates and release the hogs!' commanded Madoc. 'Proceed with care. For every injured hog, Patchwork and Snowy here will administer a scratch to each of your faces. Go on, get going!'

'But what about our bottoms?' asked Alf. 'What have we sat on? Are we going to die?'

'All in good time,' said Madoc enigmatically. 'Now get the crates out of the aircraft and start unpacking. And don't think you can run away. Amy and Minnie here have two of the best noses in the bloodhound world and they'd track you down in no time.'

Even without good noses, Alf and Gwilym would not have been difficult to trace. Alf had given up garlic, as Snowy thought he might, but the tom cat spray on the two men's trouser legs was as strong as ever. Fixit and Bill would pose no problem either, nosewise.

'We've got all your scents,' said Amy. 'There's no escape.'

'No noses to touch ours,' said Minnie, and stopped her tail in mid-wag as she heard Kip's warning growl of disapproval.

'Come on,' said Mr Fixit, 'let's do as they say or we'll all be corpses before our time.'

The four men set to work and soon the runway was alive with hedgehogs of every description. There was even an albino among them: white prickles, pale pink eyes, not so much as a black nose. Her name was Gwen, a form of *gwyn*, the Welsh word for 'white'.

Horatio was rushing round on legs that looked much longer than the cats remembered. In fact, for the first time in months, he had extended them, as hogs can, to their full ten centimetres (four inches). He greeted his relations and friends with funny snuffling sounds. 'Great Aunt Hetty! Cousin Hannibal! Sister Hyacinth! My, how you've lost weight!'

'Now can we ring for the ambulance?' demanded Mr Fixit. 'I feel that weak from the pain and I must be losing gallons of blood.'

'The poison's beginning to work. We're as good as dead if we don't get to hospital soon,' said Bill.

'Who did this to us, anyway?' asked Alf. 'And what are these spikes?'

'I feel embarrassed to let anyone see what's happened seeing where we've been spiked like,' said Gwilym, and remembered his horoscope.

'Aye, we've been made to look right fools,' added Mr Fixit. 'And we've lost our hogs, too.'

'And our money,' said Alf miserably.

'On the subject of money,' interrupted Madoc. 'You, Bill, I take it, still have the cash you were intending to hand over to Fixit for this disgraceful job.'

'Naturally,' said Bill. 'No hogs, no money. Stands to reason.'

'Paw it over! Now!' ordered Madoc in his most commanding of miaows. 'No money, no hospital, and you can all die the sort of lingering deaths these poor hogs would have suffered. Your money, Bill, or your life!'

Reluctantly, Bill drew a large pile of US dollars out of the inside breast pocket of his anorak. 'You win,' he said. 'Now, can I make a phone call?'

Alf hadn't had his question answered, so he repeated it: 'Who did this to us and what are the spikes?' he asked.

'We, the Steel Town Cats, righters of wrongs in the animal world, we planned it all and executed it,' said Madoc, sitting proudly erect, his long white whiskers fully extended.

'And the spikes?' asked Bill, still worried about being poisoned.

'Hedgehog spines,' replied Madoc. 'Every hog in the area donated one and we inserted them in the cushions while you were having your butties. Amy, Minnie and Miss Kip came along to make sure you didn't get away.'

'Hedgehog prickles,' moaned Bill. 'We'll probably get rabies or mad hedgehog disease.'

'And the money?' asked Mr Fixit. 'What are you going to do with that?'

'I'm glad you asked,' purred Madoc the Magnificent. 'I am going to divide it equally between the Cats Protection League, the National Canine Defence League and the British Hedgehog Preservation Society, worthy causes every one.'

'The phone,' moaned Bill, 'the phone.'

Chapter Fifteen

Madoc allowed Bill to phone for an ambulance. When the ambulancemen arrived and saw what the problem was they couldn't stop laughing. It was the same with the doctors and nurses at the hospital; and when the patients in the ward learned what had happened they laughed so much they forgot to switch on *Neighbours* and immediately felt much better.

In the operating theatre the prickles had to be removed surgically. Never before in medical history had such cases presented themselves and doctors and surgeons alike decided they must proceed with the greatest caution. For this reason, anaesthetic of any kind, local or general, was ruled out.

'I'm sorry, boys, but you'll just have to suffer. Bottoms up!' said the surgeon.

A veterinary surgeon was brought in to advise on prickle poisoning. He maintained it was difficult to say how toxic prickles might be, there being no data on the subject, but since you never knew where hedgehog spines might have been, the risk of blood poisoning must be high.

'Sorry, chaps, that means a big injection,' said the physician in charge of the case. 'It's similar to the rabies one, rather painful, but it's better than the alternative, don't you think?'

'Why, what's the alternative?' asked Mr Fixit.

'Well, the politically correct phrase is Negative Patient Care Outcome, in others words, death.'

'Oh dear,' said Mr Fixit. 'I don't much fancy that.'

'Well, I shouldn't worry too much,' said the physician breezily. 'The injections will almost certainly prevent an adverse situation developing. But I'm afraid that for the rest of your lives you'll be sore in the posterier region, and there's nothing we can do about that. Don't sit on hard seats or ride bicycles.'

'Ready for your injections, lads?' said a nurse. 'This will hurt you more than it hurts me.'

Outside the Accident and Emergency Unit, a queue of reporters and television cameramen waited. The story had already hit local radio.

'We're the laughing stock of the world,' moaned Mr Fixit, 'and all because of a bunch of prying cats.'

The hogs were anxious to get back to their home territory of Llanystumdwy as quickly as possible. Fortunately one of the ambulance drivers was pro-hog and he agreed to return in his car after finishing work that day and drive them there. Hogs from further afield agreed that they would like to settle in the area, too, it being famous, as Horatio assured them, for gourmet beetles, earthworms and spiders. Up until then, of course, it had been better known as the home of the great Liberal prime minister David Lloyd George, who first introduced the old-age pension.

Scarper was right about Harry the Hawk. True to his promise, he had circled overhead throughout the episode, observing the cats' progress. When he saw they had met up with Wilbert Weasel he realised his services as a guide would not be needed. Indeed, he thought it better to keep his distance high in the sky in case he was tempted to pounce on Wilbert and eat him. In different circumstances the plump little weasel would have made a tasty breakfast. Once Wilbert had left the scene, Harry came swooping down.

'Well done, cats, I saw it all. You must let my human, the Marquess, recommend you for OBEs. Or CBEs might be better: Cats of the British Empire.'

'I didn't know wild birds had humans, your Hawkship,' said Patchwork.

'Well, no, they don't really. He's not my human in the sense of looking after me, taking me to the vet and so on, but we are friends. Birds of a feather, you might say. Both interested in gardens and history. Now, is there anything I can do for you before I go? Catch a mouse or two? Fly you back to the island?'

'That's very kind of you, Harry,' said Madoc, 'but I don't think even you, as strong as you are, could carry Amy, Minnie and Miss Kip.'

'Why, how heavy are they?'

'Miss Kip is about 20 kilos and Amy and Minnie are double that.'

'No, perhaps not,' said Harry.

'But if you could fly over to Beaumaris and ask Sam to collect us . . .'

'By all means.' He shot up into the air and was

132

soon just a speck in the distance, flying along the Menai Strait in a north-westerly direction, towards Beaumaris.

When the animals got back, their humans had arranged a special feast for them in the Leisure Centre. All their favourites were there: pilchards in tomato sauce, meaty chunks in gravy, salmon heads, Cheshire cheese, tasty biscuits, bowls of cream, choc drops and, for the three dogs, a marrow bone each from Caradoc, the butcher.

'Well, Geraint, even you can't grumble at this,' said Snowy, licking his lips in anticipation.

'Spoilt for choice,' growled Geraint.

There was a mewing in the corner. It was Esmerelda and her four kittens making their first public appearance. One snow-white kitten, bigger than all the rest, rushed forward to investigate the pilchards in tomato sauce. In a second his paw had tipped over the bowl and he was covered, whiskers to tail, in thick, red liquid. He shook himself and fell into the cream, rolled over and found himself in a saucer of chocolate drops. He looked like a clown, a pierrot.

'That's my son,' purred Snowy Tom, 'a chip off the old block.'

A grey kitten with a black splodge over her eye ran up. 'You naughty kitten,' mewed her mother, 'let me lick you clean.'

'And that's a chip off the female block, the living

image of Esmerelda,' purred Snowy. 'It's good to see kittens in springtime.'

Horatio sent gruntle that all the hogs were safely back in Llanystumdwy. As predicted, Uncle Hywel had gone to the Great Hoggery in the Sky but Horatio had returned just in time to see him and give him the good news. 'Now I can go in peace,' gruntled the old hog.

The humans found it difficult to make out exactly what had happened but it was clear more legislation was needed to protect innocent wildlife. The island's member of parliament made an appointment to see Madoc at his earliest convenience. Together they would draw up a Bill which the MP would put before the House. One of the abuses he sought to stamp out was the capture of hedgehogs for export.

Tessa came to the feast with her parents, brothers and sister. It was her first outing since her illness.

'Miss Kip, you are the best dog in the world, I do love you,' she said. 'And I like your friends, Amy and Minnie. Shake paws!'

The two bloodhounds lifted enormous paws that were much bigger than Tessa's hands.

'Please love us, too,' said Amy, 'that's all we want in the world.'

'Bark,' said Minnie, and nuzzled up with an exceedingly wet nose.

As senior cat, Marmaduke sat on the platform next to the mayor. Behind him, on a high plinth, perched Harry the Hawk. It was not his custom to come indoors but he made an exception for the occasion.

'Pray silence for the Mayor of Beaumaris,' miaowed Marmaduke.

The mayor rose to his feet.

'Ladies, gentlemen, children, your Hawkship and animals,' he said. 'Our town is over 700 years old. We have a proud history, a castle, a festival and a Museum of Childhood. We also have a band of cats, the Steel Town Cats, who not only have rid this town of vermin but have championed many causes in the animal world and brought wrongdoers to justice.

Now, under their leader Madoc the Magnificent, they have solved a Prickly Problem and brought a serious loophole in the law to the attention of the authorities. It is my great pleasure, as mayor of this ancient borough, to declare the said leader, Madoc the Magnificent, prince of cats, an Honorary Burgess.'

Cameras zoomed and clicked, reporters scribbled in their notebooks and sound recordists adjusted their microphones to cat height.

'Purr, purr, purr,' said Madoc, 'multiple purrs.'